KT-474-780

By Peter Lovesey

Peter Lovesey was born in Middlesex and studied at Hampton Grammar School and Reading University, where he met his wife Jax. He won a competition with his first crime fiction novel, *Wobble to Death*, and has never looked back, with his numerous books winning and being short-listed for nearly all the prizes in the international crime writing world.

He was chairman of the Crime Writers' Association and has been presented with Lifetime Achievement awards both in the UK and the US.

For more info, visit Peter's website at www.peterlovesey.com

Peter LOVESEY

Invitation to a Dynamite Party

SPHERE

First published by Macmillan in 1974
This reissue published by Sphere in 2020

Copyright © Peter Lovesey 1974

The moral right of the author has been asserted.

A CIP catalogue record for this book is available from the British Library.

ISBN 978-0-7515-8111-9

Typeset in ITC New Baskerville by Palimpsest Book Production Ltd, Falkirk, Stirlingshire
Printed and bound in Great Britain by Clays Ltd, Elcograf S.p.A

Papers used by Sphere are from well-managed forests and other responsible sources.

Sphere
An imprint of
Little, Brown Book Group
Carmelite House
50 Victoria Embankment
London EC4Y 0DZ

An Hachette UK Company
www.hachette.co.uk

www.littlebrown.co.uk

Invitation to a Dynamite Party

1

The infernal machine lay in an underground room in the Danger Buildings of the Royal Arsenal. A sandbag structure round the inspection-bench kept observers an arm's length away. Illumination was provided by gaslight reflected through glass.

'The first time I've ever set eyes upon one,' said Detective-Sergeant Cribb, innocent of what was to come.

For all their destructive possibilities, the parts were pleasingly arranged in a metal cashbox. A cheap alarm clock from which the back had been removed. A pistol attached to it with copper wire, so that when the alarum was released, the revolving winder would be set in motion, and depress the trigger. Seven detonators ready in the box, their ends presented to the muzzle. Cakes of dynamite stacked around the side. The whole wrapped in cloth and wedged into a large leather portmanteau stuffed just as solidly with dynamite.

'It would have made an appreciable alteration to Paddington station last February if the mechanism had worked,' observed Colonel Martin, the Home Office Inspector of Explosives. A formidable crop of black whiskers covered three-quarters of his face, but his eyes were pale blue and had a wistful look.

The men from Scotland Yard visualized the scene of devastation in Mr Brunel's great glass and iron structure.

'Might I venture to inquire what prevented it from working?' asked Detective-Inspector Jowett, after a decent interval.

'Observe,' commanded the Colonel, thrusting a wooden pointer in the direction of the bomb. His companions swayed back on their heels. 'D'you see the brass plate on the back of the clock, under the gun? And d'you notice the pin at the corner? Well, gentlemen, the Great Western Railway owes the survival of its principal terminus to nothing of more consequence than that pin. It was fractionally dislodged when the bomb was put in place, and it projected far enough from the plate to check the deadly action of the alarum winder.'

'Fancy that!' said Inspector Jowett, so dedicated to the cause of personal advancement that he was ready to fancy anything a senior officer showed him. 'Merely a pin, you say. By Jove, I detect the hand of Providence in this.'

'A pity Providence was unable to prevent the explosion at Victoria station the same night,' said Colonel Martin acidly. 'Perhaps the directors of the London, Brighton and South Coast Railway should search their souls for an explanation. I tend to take a less spiritual view of things, Inspector. The working parts of an infernal machine are relatively simple to arrange, but their effectiveness depends on the proximity of a large and cumbersome mass of dynamite. When all this is encased in a portmanteau and conveyed in hazardous circumstances to the site selected for destruction, you may imagine that a delicate mechanism is liable to be displaced.'

'I can imagine it perfectly, thanks to your lucid explanation,' said Inspector Jowett.

The Colonel gave him a long look. 'Well, that is what happened at Paddington on the night of February 25th. As you probably recall—'

'Not only that,' Jowett broke in. 'Other bombs that had failed to detonate were found next day at two other stations. London Bridge and Ludgate Hill. I don't know what happened to them, but you might find it worth your while to examine them, Colonel.'

'Thank you. They are in the room behind you. Each of the alarums was set for one o'clock, the time the explosion took place in the cloakroom at Victoria. Unless you have other information, of course?'

'Not at all. Simultaneous explosions. Ugly business. There's an organization behind this, Colonel, depend upon it.'

The Colonel indicated with a slight narrowing of the eyes that the possibility had not escaped him.

'A conspiracy,' Jowett continued without check, steaming ahead on all boilers. 'No doubt about it. Dynamitards. They're here in London leaving bombs in station cloakrooms like bowler hats. Question is, Colonel, what have you discovered about 'em? You can't tell me this box of tricks hasn't furnished you with information. I know you chaps from the Home Office too well for that.'

It was unfortunately clear that Inspector Jowett did not know Colonel Martin well enough to realize he was irritating him. 'I forwarded a full report to your Special Political Branch at Scotland Yard two months ago. I suggest that you ask them to allow you to read it.'

'Ah, now there's a complication,' said Jowett, impervious to sarcasm. 'Your report might make good sense to *me*, but it is Sergeant Cribb here who will need to have the

3

information, and without disrespect to anyone I would rather that he had it first-hand. Cribb does not know it yet, but he has a privileged status, Colonel. He is in a better position to provide Scotland Yard with information about the dynamite party than the whole of the Special Branch together. We are here on the highest authority.'

Cribb listened in disbelief. The purpose of the visit was a mystery to him. Jowett had simply summoned him to the Yard, hustled him into a hansom and driven him to Woolwich. Even when they drove through the main gate he could think of no reason for being in the Arsenal.

'Very well, then,' said Colonel Martin. 'I'll address myself to you, Sergeant. What do you know about infernal machines?'

'Practically nothing, sir.'

'Hm. Better not stand so close then. No, just my joke, Sergeant, just my joke, though what the wisdom is of assigning a novice to defeat the dynamiters, I cannot begin to apprehend.'

'Nor me, sir.'

'At least we understand each other. Let's look at this contraption then, shall we?' Colonel Martin stabbed at the bomb again with his pointer. 'Cheap alarm clock, of American manufacture. Revolting name – *Peep o'Day* – wouldn't be countenanced here. Cartridge-firing pistol. Imitation Remington, but it bears no maker's imprint. Combined cap and cartridge similar to a type made at Bridgeport, Connecticut. Seven detonators containing the usual mixture of chlorate of potassium and fulminate of mercury. Simple metal cashbox with no distinguishing marks. Nothing to be gained from writing it down, Sergeant – it's all in my report. Now take a careful look at the cakes of dynamite. Don't count them – there's thirty-nine altogether – just tell me what you see on the outside.'

The Colonel's verbal dissection of the infernal machine was performed without a trace of conceit. Cribb warmed to him. 'The letter *A*, sir, and the words *Atlas Powder. A* would indicate some form of classification, I expect.'

'Good. It is the commercial mark for the highest and strongest form of dynamite. There are seven grades of the stuff manufactured by the Atlas people, at the Repauno Chemical Works, near Philadelphia. This grade contains seventy-five per cent of nitro-glycerine. Do you know what that is, Sergeant?'

'I fancy I have heard of it, but . . .'

'It is the pure form of the most powerful explosive ever developed. Two volumes of sulphuric acid, one of nitric and half of glycerine together produce a substance so devilishly liable to explode that it is virtually unusable. For twenty years scientists tried to find a means of controlling it – that is to say, exploding it with certainty under confinement. The trick was done at last in 1865 by means of a detonating cap containing fulminate of mercury, developed by a Swede, who must be a millionaire by now. He patented his nitroglycerine under the name of Nobel's Blasting Oil and sold it like hot cross buns. Trouble was that *these* buns were liable to blow up when the customers endeavoured to carry 'em home. There were some nasty accidents, gentlemen – uncommon nasty. But give Nobel his due – he persisted with his experiments until he discovered the ready means of absorbing the oil in porous substances. He tried numerous materials – paper, wood-shavings, brick-dust, clay – but none of them worked as well as a type of earth known as *Kieselguhr*, found in Hanover. It absorbed the

5

nitro-glycerine and gave it the necessary stability. He called the preparation *dynamite*. It was not so powerful as pure nitro-glycerine, but considerably safer to handle, and still a great advance on gunpowder as an explosive.'

'Anarchists and revolutionists the world over can regard Mr Nobel as their greatest benefactor, then,' said Jowett. 'A fine reputation to have!'

'Ah, but so can miners and road-builders and railway-engineers. The revolution in the civil engineering industry is far more impressive than anything your anarchists have achieved with dynamite, Inspector. Now, Sergeant, let us resume our examination of the object found on Paddington station . . .'

'A first-class bore, that Colonel Martin,' Jowett declared. 'It's always so with these forensic experts. Inspectors of explosives, pathologists, toxicologists – they're all alike. They get too close to their work, lose all perspective. I know I'm dealing with them all the time. Utterly boring. It's an experience you've been spared until today, Sergeant, getting your information from me, as you usually do.'

Cribb quietly noted the irony in the statement, and looked across the marshland towards the Thames. They were returning from the Danger Buildings to the main gate in the first-class compartment of the Arsenal train, a narrow-gauge, single-line service used for transporting personnel about the three mile extent of the grounds. The Colonel had remained behind, pleading extra investigation-work. Cribb suspected he preferred half an hour with the infernal machines to fifteen minutes more with Jowett.

It was a desolate stretch of land, broader in extent than Kensington Gardens and Hyde Park together, but without trees. The skyline was broken instead by mist-patches of varying intensity, and tall banks of earth – probably rifle-butts, but conceivably the tops of subterranean buildings. This suggestion of the other-worldly was reinforced by the occasional sighting of workers dressed identically in canvas jackets and trousers and hats with numbers attached. A group boarded the train at a stop called Mugby Junction – all third-class passengers, who had to sit back-to-back on open wagons at the rear.

'There are ten thousand or more employed here,' said Jowett, 'and they change into those clothes on arrival. There is a strict rule forbidding tobacco or matches, and anyone found disobeying it is dismissed. They have their last smoke on the way to work in the mornings and then throw away their clay pipes – which they have got free from public houses – by the entrance. I was reliably informed by the police on duty that the debris lies ankle-deep at the gate until the road-sweeper arrives each morning.'

Cribb acknowledged this information with a nod, prompted as much by the train's motion as interest in Jowett's monologue. He felt no obligation to exchange small-talk at this stage. It was high time Jowett told him the real purpose of the visit to the Arsenal. He had a right to be told, but he was damned if he would ask.

'Then there is a thriving community who live inside the Arsenal. They are mainly officers and members of the managerial staff and their families, with the servants housed in converted stables nearby. It is a veritable walled town, concentrated near the main gate, with its own shops and hospital. And the section-house, of course, for members of the Force. That's where *you* will be lodging.'

Cribb turned from the carriage-window. 'Me? What do you mean, sir?'

'Exactly as I say, Sergeant. A room has been prepared for you. I'm told it's very comfortable once you get used to the bell they ring at intervals. I have arranged for you to move in tonight. Now don't look so outraged – you might say something you'll regret. There is time for you to collect your things from your quarters and inform your dependants. The gate is locked at midnight, ten minutes after the closing-bell sounds.'

There was silence while Cribb struggled to subdue his fury and Jowett almost slavered over the exercise of his authority.

'Why should I need to lodge here?'

'The need was made abundantly clear this afternoon, Sergeant. I believe the import of what you said to Colonel Martin was that you are completely ignorant upon the subject of infernal machines. We are giving you the opportunity of becoming better informed. You will remain here until such time as the Colonel deems you sufficiently enlightened.'

It sounded like a prison sentence. 'Sufficiently for what, sir?'

'Ah. We shall come to that. You will admit, I hope, that the finer points of bomb-manufacture cannot be learned in a single afternoon. In a few weeks or so, Cribb, if you are an attentive pupil, you should graduate from this academy as the best-informed detective in the Force – upon explosives, that is.'

'Why me, sir?'

'I think we are approaching the main gate, Sergeant. Ah, now that is Dial Square, and the section-house is on the side street nearest the gate. Do you see it? That is where you report tonight. We shall shortly transfer to a cab, and I shall endeavour to answer your question on the journey back to Scotland Yard.'

'Do you recall the start of the dynamite campaign?' Jowett resumed, when their hansom was making good speed along the Woolwich Road.

Cribb drew a deep breath. Getting information from Jowett was never straightforward. 'In London, sir? I think the attempt on the Mansion House was the first, in the spring of 1882. Someone found a canister of dynamite attached to the railings.'

'Ah, yes. But the first explosion?'

'That was last year, sir, in March. The Local Government Board Offices in Charles Street.'

'Yes. Four or five rooms were totally demolished. And by a singular misfortune the building was situated opposite the headquarters of "A" Division, the King Street police station. It broke every window in the place, Cribb. The attack on *The Times* office the same night was only averted, if you recall, by the resourcefulness of a night-watchman with a bucket of water. That night's doings more than anything else precipitated the passing of the new Explosives Act. Then, three weeks later, public confidence was restored by a timely police success, the discovery of the nitro-glycerine manufactory at Birmingham and the arrest of the infamous Dr Gallagher and his fellow-conspirators. It confirmed what many had suspected – that the dynamitards were Irish-Americans, and the campaign a ruthless attempt to bring the issue of Home Rule before the public – possibly even to intimidate the Government into yielding to the Irish faction. You haven't any Irish blood in your family, have you, Sergeant?'

'No, sir.'

'Excellent. Not that one questions your loyalty, of course. We cannot over-estimate the dangers involved in this business. If a certain detective in Birmingham had not had his suspicions aroused by the behaviour of the man Whitehead, the chemist of the plotters, and visited him in disguise, we might well have seen the swift destruction of many of London's finest edifices. There was enough nitro-glycerine there to demolish every street in the City of London, Cribb. He was consigning it to the Metropolis in india-rubber fishing-boots contained in packing-cases. The others, who frequented small hotels and retired lodgings in the south of London, were arrested before they could carry out their frightful work. Gallagher himself, the brains of the conspiracy, had travelled over first-class in the Cunarder *Parthia* and was living as a gentleman in the Strand, if you can credit that. He and three others were given penal servitude for life. And there the matter ended, until the two explosions on the Underground Railway last October. Railway property was seriously damaged. The cost of repairs amounted to several thousand pounds, did you know that? I believe a number of passengers were maimed for life by the Praed Street explosion as well – only men of the labouring-class, but no less worthy of our pity for that, Sergeant. Incidents of that sort impress the populace. The newspapers made a good deal of it. Fears were revived, Sergeant, fears were revived.'

'More so by the explosion at Victoria in February,' added Cribb, with an interest in bringing the catalogue briskly up to date. 'And the simultaneous attempts on London Bridge, Paddington and Ludgate Hill.'

'What did you say?' said Jowett, still mentally at Praed Street. 'Ah, yes, indeed. The railway station outrages. Well, the dynamite party unwittingly did you a good turn, Sergeant, leaving three unexploded machines for us to take to Woolwich and dismantle. You cannot expect to have such good fortune again, however. Next time, the disagreeable things are sure to go off.'

Cribb decided it was time to correct the impression that he had a personal stake in the dynamite campaign. 'I'm confident that the Special Branch has allowed for that, sir. Some of the best detectives in the Force were conscripted for it. Best leave it all to them, I say.'

'The Special Branch,' Jowett repeated distantly. 'A hand-picked group of detectives brought together for the sole purpose of combating the dynamitards. They occupy the room next to mine. I had to give them my telephone-set and two of my clerical assistants. Most inconvenient. Brand-new desks and stools and a hatstand of their own. Someone in high authority is exceedingly exercised about all this, Cribb.'

'I'm not surprised, sir. Who's to say where the next bomb might be placed? For a party of Irish-Americans just off the boat, these dynamiters have an uncanny knack of setting their machines down in public places without being noticed. Each of those stations was well patrolled. And you know how it is with railway station patrols – one constable is always assigned to watch the comings and goings at the cloakroom. What with trunk murders and stolen property and anarchists' black bags, you need to keep an eye on everyone who approaches the counter. How four large cases containing bombs were deposited the same night at four stations without anyone having any recollection of who left them, I can't fathom.'

Jowett nodded his agreement. 'I suppose one must accept that constables on duty are not infallible. There is the possibility, for example, of some person unknown chancing to deliver an infernal machine to the cloakroom in the interval between reliefs, when the new relief are being marched to their beats, but it is quite inconceivable that such a thing could have happened at four stations on one evening. Unless, of course, the dynamite party got to know the times at which the reliefs were changed.'

Cribb was sceptical. 'Not likely, in my estimation, sir. The recent practice is to vary the reliefs from week to week. One week they might change over at six, the next half past. It's all arranged by the divisional Inspectors. The information isn't given to the men themselves until a day or two before. The dynamiters couldn't possibly have known it without the co-operation of one of the Force. And that, sir, would mean that we were harbouring an informer.'

Cribb fully expected Jowett to consider the suggestion as scandalous and outrageous as a bare head at Ascot, or braces in the Boat Race. Instead, he lifted his forefinger in front of him in a gesture pregnant with significance.

'Exactly what I was coming to, Sergeant. What would you say if I told you that one of the Force – one of the Detective Department, indeed – had been seen in the company of Irish-Americans in a public house shortly before the explosion at the Local Government Board, and again before the attacks on the railway stations?'

'I should find it difficult to believe, sir – unless there was some explanation. Perhaps the officer concerned was a member of the Special Branch.'

'He was not, Sergeant. Nor did he record any account of the meetings in his daily diary.'

'Then I should want an explanation, sir,' decided Cribb. 'I should call him in and ask him to give an account of himself.'

Jowett smiled in a superior way. 'Doubtless you would, Sergeant, doubtless you would. It seems the obvious thing to do. However, the obvious thing is not necessarily the most productive of results. If we call the officer in and question his behaviour, the word will not be long in reaching his American associates. Dismissing this man from the Force would be a poor exchange for keeping in contact with the dynamitards, if dynamitards they be.'

Cribb frowned, and said nothing, not a little shocked at the deviousness of what Jowett was suggesting.

The Inspector seemed to read his thoughts. 'You must understand that we are not dealing with petty thieves or one of your backyard murderers, Cribb. We are fighting a secret society pledged to wrench Ireland from Her Majesty's dominion by every means at its disposal. It is better organized and better financed than any Irish conspiracy this century. It is known as the Clan-na-Gael. Its membership in America runs to thousands, Sergeant, thousands, all organized into numerous subordinate bodies, or *camps*. The dynamitards are emissaries of the Clan, trained men picked for their daring and knowledge of explosives and sent here to mount a campaign of terror and destruction. Faced with a conspiracy on such a scale as that, we are not going to pounce on the one policeman whose erratic behaviour may help us to defeat the Clan. He will be dealt with when his usefulness to us is over, you may be assured.'

Cribb was floundering. He knew nothing of secret societies. Wasn't there said to be a War Office Intelligence

Department to deal with such things? 'Might I enquire what connection this has got with me, sir?'

'Indeed you may, Sergeant. You have been nominated to make contact with the constable in question and win his confidence.'

'Me, sir?'

'If you perform your duties well, Cribb, you may be the first agent to penetrate the dynamite conspiracy in London.'

'*Agent?*' repeated Cribb, eyes agape.

'No more than a word, Sergeant. I can promise you that the whole of the Special Branch is deeply interested in the outcome of your mission. You will function independently of them, however, and remain responsible to me. It is at my suggestion that you are to be educated in the science of explosives. The closer one gets to the dynamitards, the more necessary it becomes to understand their diabolical machines. Do you follow me?'

'I'm not sure, sir. Are you proposing that I should infiltrate the dynamite conspiracy by befriending the constable who is suspected of being an informer?'

'Exactly so, Cribb. And to anticipate your next question, the reason why you have been selected is that you already know the constable in question better than anybody else in the Force. He is your sometime super-numerary and satellite, Detective-Constable Thackeray.'

2

Long after the cab put them down in Great Scotland Yard, Cribb was deep in conversation with Inspector Jowett. For the first time that day he functioned as a detective. He was totally involved in acquiring information, and he subjected Jowett to the class of interrogation usually reserved for the last suspect in a case of murder. He discharged a volley of questions at the hapless inspector under the blue lamp at the very entrance to the police offices. Nothing in the case against Thackeray escaped his attention. He extracted the evidence the Special Branch had amassed syllable by syllable. Only when he had recorded it all in his notebook and had it checked again by Jowett did he allow him to pass inside. Then, still studying the notes, he walked slowly across the Yard and along Northumberland Avenue in the direction of the Embankment.

There, by the Thames, where he and Thackeray had so often plotted the arrest of dangerous men, Cribb pondered his assistant's strange conduct. *Strange* – it was unbelievable that a constable who had faced corpses, crocodiles, even naked chorus girls, in the name of law and order should so abandon his principles as to consort with the dynamite party. Thackeray an informer? Thackeray the lion-hearted, the man above all others he would have at his side in an emergency? Monstrous.

Yet as he stood at the Embankment wall and regarded the river – not the steam-launches and sailing-barges, nor the beguiling glitter of afternoon sunlight, but the water itself below him, turbid and thick with impurities, flowing more rapidly than ever it appeared from a cursory glance across the surface – Cribb decided to re-examine his opinion of Thackeray. It took several more minutes' contemplation of the water to achieve the detachment to penetrate the layers of loyalty and regard formed in five years. What was then revealed – what he *really* knew of the man – was so slight that he winced at the realization.

He called himself a detective and all he knew about his principal assistant was that he stood six feet tall in his socks, sported a grey beard and was game for anything except educational classes. Exaggeration, perhaps, but not short of the truth. Oh, there were other details – the fondness for melodrama and Kop's ale, the tender feet and the sensitiveness upon the subject of retirement – but what did they amount to? What grounds had he for believing Thackeray incorruptible? The plain truth was that the section-house adjoining Paradise Street police station could be a dynamite manufactory for all he knew. Not once had he met Thackeray off duty. He had no idea whether he was a Home Ruler or a hot gospeller. The man was dependable when it mattered, and that had always been enough.

He supposed he ought to examine the divisional defaulters' book. Thackeray's name would be there, for sure. There was not a constable of any length of service whose sheet was blank. *Entries on the defaulter sheet in the first years of service*, said the *Police Code*, *will materially reduce the possibility of eventual promotion and selection for the prizes of the Force* – so every station inspector took it as his duty to foster discipline among young constables by including their names from time to time in the Morning Report. Nor were the not-so-young forgotten: *If a man's conduct has not been uniformly good, or his incapacity may have been brought about by irregular or vicious habits, the Commissioner will recommend that a lower scale of pension or gratuity be granted to him.* In his more bitter moments, when the prizes of the Force seemed too remote to bother over, Cribb would point out that even if one earned a commendation (and there was no regular procedure for that) the only place where it could be recorded was on the defaulter sheet.

So Thackeray's sheet would contain the predictable catalogue of misdemeanours – taking off the armlet to obtain a drink from a publican, gossiping on duty, quarrelling with comrades, soliciting gratuities, unpunctuality, and so on – together with a list of the stations he had served in, and perhaps an entry in red ink commending his part in the arrest of Charles Peace in 1878. Cribb doubted if there would be any subsequent entries in red; none of the crimes he and Thackeray had investigated had caused such a stir.

He thought of going down to Rotherhithe to find out what the Paradise Street contingent knew of Thackeray. There must be someone who had an off-duty drink with him, or lodged in the section-house. You could hardly use the same scullery and tin bath without getting to know something about a man. He considered the idea, and rejected it.

This was his dilemma – the repugnance he felt at being asked to spy on Thackeray, and the necessity of discovering what the man was doing. Until he was sure of Thackeray's complicity, he refused to ignore the bond between them – however slender it suddenly seemed. For Jowett, though, the issue had been clear. 'The Yard recognizes that some of its employees are corrupt,' he had blandly explained. 'What do you expect on a wage of seventy-eight pounds a year for a constable, First Class? Read your *Police Gazette*, Sergeant. It is full of wretched officers who have succumbed to bribery of one sort or another. There are just as many dismissed constables – not to speak of sergeants – scrubbing out workhouses as there are inspectors such as myself promoted for unstinting service. That is the nature of our profession, Cribb. Thackeray has misguidedly transgressed, and must prepare to join the floor-scrubbers. Not before he has rendered certain services to the dynamite investigation, however. You are not, on any account, to inform him of what we know.'

There was nothing for it but to co-operate. If Thackeray were really an informer, Cribb could only believe it by seeing it for himself. If not – if he were innocent and shamefully misrepresented – the way to set the record straight was to learn what was going on. Either way, Cribb was now drawn in to the dynamite investigation, and the threat to public safety overshadowed everything. He was committed to a course of action totally repugnant to him – spying on Thackeray, decent, dutiful, dependable Thackeray.

'Damn you, Thackeray!' he said aloud, and instantly felt better for it.

He left the Embankment thinking not of his assistant, but Mrs Cribb, and how she would take the news of his move to Woolwich Arsenal.

* * *

18

The course in explosives, Cribb shortly discovered, was organized with Civil Service precision. A team of Home Office experts and sergeant-instructors from the Royal Artillery engaged his attention continuously between 7 a.m. and 9 p.m. each day. As their solitary trainee, he stood in solemn attendance while they mounted their set-pieces, lit the fuses, and retired. Sometimes the preliminaries took two or three hours, but the conversation was entirely confined to such things as time-fuses and percussion-caps. The instructors shrank from anything more sociable. Between detonations they allowed him to eat or sleep. Any remaining time – and there was precious little of it – was expected to be spent practising with firearms on the ranges. By the week's end he was almost ready to doubt whether observation of the Sabbath was permitted to secret agents under instruction.

It required unimaginable self-discipline to raise himself from his pillow on the Sunday, his head still singing from a Litho-fracteur blast and his shoulder sore from rifle-practice, and examine a telegraph message from Inspector Jowett: *Thackeray off duty today. Suggest you keep under discreet observation.* Did this mean no explosions were planned that day? He was into his clothes and out of the Arsenal gates before anyone could tell him otherwise.

A train to Liverpool Street and a cab across London Bridge brought him to Rotherhithe, and Paradise Street police station. The sergeant on duty was an old friend.

'Thackeray? Reliable man. Helped to arrest Charlie Peace in seventy-eight, did you know that?'

'He's helped me too, on occasions,' said Cribb, a little bleakly. 'Where do I find him this morning – in the section-house?'

'I doubt it. He's an early riser. He'll have been up since six. Thackeray doesn't believe in spending his time here when he can be up and about. Not lately, anyway.'

Cribb noted the emphasis. 'He's changed his habits, you mean?'

There was a shade too much of the professional manner in the inquiry. The duty sergeant shot him a quick glance. He felt the shabbiness of what he was doing.

'He goes out a bit more, that's all,' explained the sergeant. 'I don't believe in prying into a man's off-duty hours.'

'Nor me,' said Cribb emphatically. 'A bobby's entitled to his private life, as much as any member of the public. Do you know the duty I shirk more than any other? Inspecting the lodgings once a month. It's a liberty going into a man's home uninvited, in my opinion. No, I was wanting to see Thackeray for old time's sake. We've worked together so often, you understand. You wouldn't know where I could find him, I suppose?' This was altogether more casual and disarming.

'Sunday morning?' said the sergeant. 'Probably at one of the main railway stations. He spends a lot of his time at the stations, if my information's correct.'

Cribb gulped.

'I'll ask if anyone knows,' the sergeant continued. 'I wouldn't want to send you to Paddington if he's fixed on Waterloo this time.'

The constable at the desk thought Thackeray had set off in the direction of London Bridge.

'I'll try that, then,' said Cribb, quickly. 'You wouldn't know what he *does* at the main line stations, would you?'

'I've no idea, Sergeant. He don't talk to nobody about it.'

Cribb thanked them, and took a bus up Jamaica Road and Tooley Street, a mile's drive along the riverside, past breweries and warehouses. To the left, trains thundered along the viaduct above the chimney-pots of Bermondsey.

He left the bus at a step brisk enough to betray anxiety about the future of London Bridge station. Thackeray was not in the booking-hall. Nor had the man in the cloakroom seen anyone answering his description that morning. His step eased a little.

Eventually he discerned a familiar, bearded figure in bowler hat and ulster at the far end of the Brighton platform. He purchased a platform ticket and strode straight up to his man. Discreet observation be blowed!

Thackeray had not noticed his approach. 'Good Lord! You, Sarge? Fancy that!'

'I saw you standing there,' said Cribb, truthfully, 'so I came along.'

'What are you doing, then? Are you off to Brighton for the day?'

'Not me,' said Cribb. 'How about you?'

A tinge of mild embarrassment coloured the constable's cheeks. 'Me, Sarge? I-er-well, if you really want to know, I'm here because of this.' He made a small, limp gesture with his hand.

Cribb's eyes followed the direction, and then blinked. '*That*, you mean?'

Thackeray nodded.

In his bee-line along the platform, Cribb had quite omitted to notice it: an enormous express locomotive painted in the brilliant golden ochre and dark olive green livery of the London, Brighton and South Coast Railway Company.

'Number 214,' Thackeray said, as if he were making an introduction. 'The *Gladstone*. One of William Stroudley's engines.'

Cribb nodded, avoiding the impulse to lift his hat.

'Did you ever see such a finish?' Thackeray went on, with undisguised emotion. 'Look at that buffer-beam, Sarge. There's all of five colours in it – red, white, black, yellow and claret. And how about the wheels – ain't they the handsomest that ever touched a track? What other railway company would paint its wheel-centres bright yellow and keep 'em as clean as that?' He turned on Cribb, almost challenging him to supply an answer.

The sergeant frowned. 'Do I understand, Thackeray, that you came here this morning to make the acquaintance of this – er – Number 214? To a railway terminus, on your day off?'

'I couldn't have seen her anywhere else, Sarge,' said Thackeray simply. 'And she's worth a mile walk on a Sunday morning, you must admit. Mr Stroudley hasn't any rivals as a locomotive-engineer, in my opinion.'

'I'll take your word for it. Just hadn't pictured you pacing railway platforms in your spare time. Is this a new enthusiasm?' Cribb said it rather as a doctor inquires about the onset of an illness.

'I've been going to stations on my days off since the October before last,' Thackeray admitted. 'It first gripped me on the Brighton line when we was returning from the Prothero investigation. We was pulled by 328, if you recall, the *Sutherland*, one of the G class. She was only single-drive, but when I saw her as we came up the platform, standing there so nobby with the steam still rising from her, something happened inside me, Sarge. A kind of fluttering in my stomach. I've been unable to pass a station ever since.'

'Must be inconvenient,' said Cribb. 'You weren't here on the morning they found the infernal machine, I suppose?'

Thackeray shook his head. 'No, more's the pity. What a diabolical thing to do, putting a bomb in a station! I saw the damage caused by the one at Victoria. It wrecked half a dozen offices and shattered the glass roof, as well as bursting the gas-pipes and starting a sizeable fire. Someone will have to catch these dynamiters soon. The Special Branch don't seem to be making much progress, if the talk at Paradise Street can be relied upon. I'd like to know how that lot spend their time.'

Watching you, thought Cribb. He decided to change the topic. 'Where do you drink these days, Thackeray? Now that we've chanced to meet in this way, I'd like to buy you a pint of ale, if you weren't planning to spend the rest of the day with Number 214, that is.'

The constable grinned sheepishly. 'She has to be off in a few minutes, as it happens, Sarge. Twelve-thirty to Brighton, via Victoria and East Croydon. She's the fast.'

'Ah, then I shall definitely take you for a drink,' said Cribb. 'Best to leave the fast ones alone, eh? Which pub did you say?'

'*The Feathers* in Rotherhithe, Sarge. Just a halfpenny bus ride away. I'm the only one from Paradise Street that drinks there. The others go to the *Spread Eagle*. They're a trifle particular about where they drink in view of all the bother lately. Mine's an Irish pub, you see.'

It had to be, thought Cribb, inwardly groaning. How many more connections would Thackeray have with the dynamite campaign? Any minute now he was going to mention the Peep o'Day alarm clock an American friend had given him, and the imitation Remington pistol he kept in a portmanteau under his bed.

'It ain't the best time for service,' Thackeray explained, as they approached *The Feathers*. 'We shan't get near the pump for brats.' But his substantial form moved like an ironclad through the throng of ragged infants clamouring with jugs for the noonday beer for their families. 'Two swipes, Michael,' he called over the cropped heads, and in seconds the Yard was slaking its thirst at a table in the corner.

After a long draught, Cribb cordially asked, 'How's the crime in Rotherhithe, then?'

'I'd be obliged if you'd keep your voice down, Sarge,' said Thackeray through his teeth. 'I don't like to be known here as one of the Force. The crime? Ah, it's about the same, you know. There ain't much to talk of – not that you'd cross the road for, so to speak. The usual brawling in the docks. It provides me with a stabbing or a question-able drowning once or twice a week to occupy my time. Otherwise I'm left with fallen women and ferocious dogs. Oh, and opium-smokers. We've got as many Chinamen between here and London Bridge as there is in Pekin. What's the matter with your right arm, Sarge?'

Cribb patted the area of his collar-bone, so sore from rifle-practice that he was drinking left-handed. 'Too much responsibility,' he joked. 'It's more than I can shoulder.'

'Do you need some assistance?' Thackeray spoke in earnest, shaming the sergeant with open-heartedness.

'No, no. Nothing like that. So this is an Irish house, then. Didn't know you favoured the Paddies – or is it the hard stuff that you've taken a fancy to?'

24

'Not me, Sarge. I never was a whisky man. No, I come here for my own reasons – professional reasons, you might say. I've never forgotten something you told me the first time we worked together. There's more useful information to be learned in a public taproom than there is in the *Police Gazette.*'

'Did I say that? Must have been feeling low at the time, Thackeray.'

'Ah, but there's a deal of truth in it. Provided that you don't spend your time drinking with bobbies, that is. There's nothing so certain to put a stop to conversation in a pub as half a dozen pairs of regulation boots crossing the threshold. I think you said that, too, Sarge.'

'Probably.' Cribb took another draught. 'You still haven't told me why you drink in an Irish pub.'

Thackeray leaned forward confidentially. 'That's something I wouldn't care to go in to this morning, Sarge.'

'Dangerous company these days, the Irish,' Cribb persisted. 'They've other things on their minds than Blarney Stones and fairy cobblers. Do you just listen, or do you mix with 'em?'

'A bit of both, I suppose. You can't sit in a corner on your own and say nothing. That would give them cause for suspicion, wouldn't it? I pass the time of day to anyone that catches my eye, and if they want to say a few words more, well I don't turn my back on them.'

'Do you buy 'em a drink?'

'On my wage? Not unless they buy one first for me.'

Cribb nodded. 'I take your point. My turn to fill the glasses. You'll have another?'

'Since it's my day off, yes. My first Sunday in three months.'

'These drinking-companions of yours,' Cribb doggedly began again, when he returned with the beer. 'The ones that treat you first, I mean. Are any of 'em here this morning?'

'Not many do, Sarge. We tend to buy our own. It's more likely to be the occasional visitor that treats you than the regulars. Good health.'

'Yours, too. Who would want to come to a pub like this – without disrespect, of course – in the backstreets of Rotherhithe, and stand a round of drinks for a bunch of Irish dockers and a constable off duty?'

'They don't know about *me*, Sarge,' Thackeray assured him in a whisper. 'Someone with a sharp ear for accents might detect that I wasn't born in Tipperary, but they don't know I'm in the Force. If there's a round of drinks being bought, I'm usually included. I was personally treated once, too.'

'Who by?'

Thackeray smiled. 'Ah, a big, bearded American with more money than sense. He came here three or four months ago, early in the new year. Swore he was an Irishman whose family emigrated at the time of the potato famine.'

'Did he have an Irish name?'

'I don't recall, Sarge. We was conversing about trains, and once I'm on that subject I find that I don't listen much to the other fellow. He wasn't what you might call a railway connoisseur, but he was interested. He kept asking questions about railway stations and buying me whisky.'

Jerusalem! Cribb blinked. 'You were on spirits that night, then?'

'I have a nip just occasional, Sarge. Yes, he was a generous sort of cove. Big, too. Barge-horse of a man. Stood well over six foot. None of the regulars would have wanted to mix it with him.'

'Was he a fighting man, then?'

'I don't think so. I always look at the hands, since you taught me how to spot a pugilist. It was odd, really. There was hard skin on them, and some blistering, but it was on the palms, not the knuckles.'

'A navvy,' suggested Cribb.

'Not with money to spend on whisky, Sarge. Besides, I looked at the fingernails, and they were *manicured*. You notice a thing like that in a dockers' pub.'

'I'm sure.'

'Another thing,' said Thackeray, clearly experiencing a total recollection. 'His hands smelt of spirits.'

'Whisky, you mean?'

'No, Sarge. Methylated. Strange, I do remember his name now. It came back to me with the smell. Malone.'

'Malone. Did he happen to mention how long he was staying in London?'

'No, but I could ask his friends. There's three or four over from America who visit *The Feathers* regular.'

'Three or four?' Cribb sank the rest of his beer at a gulp. 'Perhaps you'd care to tell me about *them*. I need another drink first.'

And fast. Three or four! Lord, it was like being beaten over the head with a truncheon. Or a shillelagh. The innocence of the man!

When the descriptions were done, and they stood outside in the street looking for a cab for Cribb, Thackeray seemed at last to sense his concern. 'I wouldn't want you to think me unco-operative, Sarge,' he said, 'but I've never really had the opportunity of doing much detective-work on my own. You know how it is when you overhear something that just *might* have some connection with a matter under investigation. You keep it to yourself until you've got something positive, or you find that it don't mean a thing. These blooming Irish have such fanciful notions that if you believed everything they said, you wouldn't stop another night in London. It's sorting out what's the truth that takes the time. But I can wait. I have to win their confidence first.'

'That's the dangerous bit,' said Cribb.

'What do you mean?'

'The easiest way to gain a confidence is to give one.'

'I'm not sure what you're saying, Sergeant.'

Confound the man. He could not put it more plainly. 'Think about it, Thackeray. Think about it. There's no more difficult duty in police work than handling an informant correct. That's another dictum to remember. Do you understand me?'

Thackeray looked at Cribb for several seconds. Then he nodded his head once. His face was expressionless. It was as if an empty frame signalled the end of a lantern-show.

3

Cribb's course at the Arsenal ended in an unexpected way early on 31 May 1884.

The sound of the morning mug of tea arriving on his locker was followed by a deferential cough. 'Your beverage, Sergeant,' a voice announced, 'and if you would be so decent as to down it at your earliest convenience –'

What the devil! He turned his head on the pillow.

'– you'll be ready for the van which is already on its way from Scotland Yard for you,' continued the duty constable, a mealy-mouthed member of the Woolwich establishment he had scarcely noticed before. 'I was most particularly instructed to rouse you and advise you in a civil manner to be packed and ready to leave by six. Begging your pardon, Sergeant.'

Scotland Yard? The fellow might have said Timbuctoo for all the significance it had at 5.30 a.m., three weeks into the explosives course. He groped for the programme on his locker. 'It's Saturday. Blast effects and craters. I have it written here.'

'Yes, Sergeant. The platoon has already passed through the gates on its way to dynamite the demonstration area.'

Cribb gripped the sides of the bed. 'Then what the blazes are you going on about police vans for?'

'Orders from the Yard, Sergeant. A telegraph from Inspector Jowett arrived during the night. They want you urgently.'

If Jowett had got up in the night to send a telegraph, the urgency was extreme.

'Then you'd better stop the platoon before it starts the dynamiting.'

'I couldn't do that, Sergeant, with respect. That's an army matter. We have no authority to interfere in army matters.'

'Confound it, man, they'll be doing their dynamiting for nothing. I shan't be here.'

'Ah, but they'll still need the craters.'

'Whatever for?'

'Filling in, Sergeant. There's a fatigue-party laid on for this afternoon. They parade at half past twelve, draw spades from the store at one o'clock and commence filling in at a quarter past. I stand to be corrected, but I don't think the army would appreciate having to change all that on the Saturday before the Whitsun holiday.'

Cribb took a mouthful of tea. 'Why should I agitate myself about the army anyway? Get me some toast and dripping, lad. I'm damned sure Jowett hasn't invited me to the Yard for breakfast.'

The journey there confirmed that impression. It was not the kind of jaunt that kindled the stomach-juices. The van-driver took the streets of Greenwich and Deptford at the gallop, as if all the cat's meat men and milk-boys were Red Indians in ambush. Cribb, inside, braced himself grimly against the seat-back and tried to imagine what exigency justified such driving.

There was a marked slowing of the pace after Westminster

Bridge, not unconnected, Cribb decided, with the fact that they were now in 'A' Division, the home of the Yard itself. But the driver disabused him of that notion by saying through the communication-window: 'Sorry about the hold-up, Sergeant. The traffic's jammed all the way along Whitehall. It'll be the crowds ahead, I reckon.'

Crowds? Before eight in the morning on Saturday in Whitehall? Who could they be – Socialists? Suffragists? Extraordinary time for a public demonstration.

'You'd be just as quick on foot, if I might suggest it,' the driver went on. 'It'll take us twenty minutes this way.'

He was right. It would be quicker to foot it, so long as he didn't find himself in the thick of a demonstration. 'What's going on this morning?' he asked.

'Sight-seers, I reckon, Sergeant. There was a crowd already gathering in the Yard when I left soon after six this morning.'

Cribb had never regarded Great Scotland Yard as one of the sights of London. Visitors from the provinces occasionally called at the Convict Office and in return for a small contribution to police funds were taken up to the garret to see a collection of grisly relics that had come to be known as the Criminal Museum, but the Yard itself was otherwise one of the dullest spots in the capital – until this morning, apparently. Well, he was damned if he would ask the van-driver a second time what was going on. 'I shall make my way on foot, then, Constable.'

'Very well, Sergeant. Inspector Jowett said you was to report to him in his usual office.'

Confounded cheek, telling him where to report, as if Jowett had ever said such a thing. Some of these drivers seemed to think that managing a pair of horses successfully gave them a privileged position in the Force. Why, a man like Thackeray had never breathed an insubordinate word in all the time he had known him, yet here was this jumped-up stable-lad coolly giving orders to a sergeant after driving him across London at a rate that could only be described as hair-raising.

He was glad of the walk to cool his temper a little. The way he felt on leaving the van, he was liable to say something to Jowett he might regret. Besides, he was actually making quicker progress than the line of vehicles. Some of the cab-men had resignedly attached nosebags to their horses' heads. But his fellow-pedestrians interested him more than the traffic. There were more travelling in his direction than one usually encountered, and by no means all were Civil Servants on their way to work. By their appearance, many were members of the poor class who had trooped across Westminster Bridge from the backstreets of Lambeth, some in considerable groups, children, parents and grandparents marching purposefully up Whitehall, bright-eyed with the expectation of some family treat in store.

At a loss to account for it, Cribb strode briskly on until the press of people beyond the Horse Guards slowed him to a shuffle. The Yard itself, when he reached it, was as thick with humanity as a painting by Frith. The concourse had come to an enforced stop. They stood shoulder to shoulder, bowler to bowler. Infants sat astride their fathers' backs and snatched at the tassels of passing parasols. Newspaper-boys and fruit-sellers had materialized from nowhere and bawled their wares into the captive ears around them.

Being tall, Cribb could glimpse the helmets of a police

cordon controlling the crowd. He pressed forward with difficulty. It was some minutes before he reached the front ranks. There, the reason for the crowd's presence came dramatically in sight.

A hole about fifteen feet by twenty had been blasted in the Criminal Investigation Department. Debris was scattered widely across the quadrangle, amongst it broken cupboards, a battered safe and the remains of two carriages, a landau and a brougham. The front of the *Rising Sun*, on the opposite side, was in ruins, although the landlord had contrived an entrance for the public, who were paying to look inside. Every window in the Yard had been shattered by the explosion. Workmen were engaged in shoring up the Police Office with wooden beams.

Cribb reached the police-line, was recognized, and passed through, stepping over the rubble with a sureness of foot quite recently acquired. The entrance was on the side away from the explosion. He mounted the stairs to Jowett's office.

'Kindly leave the door open behind you,' the Inspector called to him as he went in. 'We shall at least be able to breathe if there is an unobstructed passage of air. This dust is asphyxiating me by degrees.' He was seated at his usual desk in front of a window-frame empty except for a few jagged segments of glass. A large fall of plaster from the ceiling had all but obliterated the tufted rug to which, as a senior officer, he was entitled. A thin film of white dust lay over everything in the room, including his hair and suit. 'Unfortunately, there is nowhere else for us to talk.'

'When did this happen, sir?'

'Shortly after nine o'clock last night. One of the newspapers has already produced a special edition to report it. I have been here myself since the small hours.' He stroked the unshaven bristles on his chin to emphasize his quick response to the emergency. 'They sent a cab out to South Norwood for me.'

Better than a police-van, thought Cribb. 'Is this the work of the Clan-na-Gael, sir?'

'Without a shadow of doubt. Did you notice which room was the target of the attack?'

'It looked to me like the Hackney Carriage Licensing Department, sir.'

'No, on the upper floor. It is the room next to this, the new headquarters of the Special Irish Branch. They have struck directly at the officers who are investigating them. If that isn't the Clan snapping its fingers in our faces, I don't know what is.'

'Was anyone hurt, sir?'

'Several. None fatally, we think. P.C. Clarke, the constable on duty in the Yard, was blown against a wall and suffered a severe scalp wound. Six others, including a coachman and the barmaid from the *Rising Sun*, are in Charing Cross Hospital. Mercifully, no one was in the office at the time. It is extensively damaged, as you may imagine.' Jowett paused, and frowned. 'I have not seen inside, but I doubt whether my telephone-set has survived.'

'I'm sorry, sir. One other point: I wouldn't wish to criticize a man in no position to defend himself, but if P.C. Clarke was on duty in the Yard, how was it that he didn't notice the infernal machine before it exploded?'

'A perfectly proper observation, Cribb. The answer is that it was not in view. The dynamitards had secreted it in what one might describe as a convenient hiding-place adjoining the wall of the building.'

'Oh? What was that, sir?' said Cribb, blankly.

Jowett looked embarrassed and ran his hand over the back of his head, producing a small halo of dust. 'Well, not to beat about the bush . . .'

'Ah! The public urinal, sir! Perfectly sited for their devilish purpose.'

'Exactly so.'

'That would account for the blast effects,' said Cribb, pleased to air his new expertise. 'The vertical thrust of the blast quite surprised me. The bricks have been displaced to a height of up to twenty feet. The urinal acted like a cannon, you see. Instead of the force being dispersed in all directions from the point of detonation, it was concentrated upwards. Curious – I was due for a practical demonstration of blast effects this morning. I didn't know the Clan was going to provide it for me.'

'You have not seen all that they provided,' said Jowett.

'What do you mean, sir?'

'There were two other explosions last night, in St James's Square. The Junior Carlton Club was attacked at eighteen minutes past nine. Fifteen seconds after, there was a second explosion across the Square, at Sir Watkin Wynn's residence.'

'A private residence? What have they got against Sir Watkin Wynn?'

'Nothing at all. It was patently a mistake. The target must have been Winchester House next door, which is government property.'

'And the Junior Carlton Club?'

'Now that is interesting.' Jowett opened a book on his desk. 'This is a copy of the *London Directory*. In the section on St James's Square there is no mention of the club. You see, its front entrance is in Pall Mall, and the back, in the

Square, is used by tradesmen and servants. A foreigner to London might well turn to the *Directory* as an authority and gain the impression that the back entrance of the club, which is indistinguishable from any other mansion, is, in fact, Adair House, the home of the War Office Intelligence Department.'

'Good Lord! The Special Branch and the Secret Service on one night! These fellows don't do things by halves. What was the damage in St James's Square?'

'Mostly superficial, I am glad to report. It is miraculous that nobody was killed. The parts of the Junior Carlton occupied by members were almost untouched, but the kitchen and the servants' quarters suffered somewhat. The bomb had been left at the foot of an iron staircase leading to the basement. The second bomb, at Sir Watkin Wynn's, shattered all the windows there and in the Duke of Cleveland's mansion next door, but the fullest force of the impact was curiously diverted at an angle of ninety degrees to Adair House. It brought down the mortar and dashed out the windows with such a powerful concussion that for a time it was believed there had been three explosions in the Square.'

'That's a nobby area, sir. Railway stations are one thing, noble residences quite another.'

'Don't I know it! Our list of witnesses reads like *Burke's Peerage*. Unfortunately, they all appeared *after* the explosions. Now, Cribb, I have something more to show you, but I am interested to know what your observations are thus far, coming fresh from the explosives course, as you do.'

Fresh was not the word he would have used to describe his condition after three weeks at Woolwich. 'I would need to see the places where the bombs were placed, sir. Possibly

I could tell you then which method of detonation was used. The remnants of a clock-timing device are nearly always detectable at the place where the charge has exploded.'

'Yes, yes. But what have you got to say about the organization of the crime?'

What was he coming to? Best tread warily. 'Well-planned, I should say, sir, allowing that there seem to have been some mistakes in St James's Square. Possibly the perpetrators were less efficient than the plotters. Friday evening was a good one to choose.'

'To have the maximum effect upon the populace over the bank holiday? You're right, of course. The Local Government Board explosion last year coincided with the Easter holiday, if I remember. Everyone came out to watch, as they will this weekend.'

'There's also the question of the Oaks, sir.'

'The Oaks? What has a blasted horse-race got to do with it?'

'The number of constables withdrawn for duty at Epsom, sir. We're always under-staffed on Oaks Day. It's a thing an Irishman might think of.'

'An Irish-American?'

'I wouldn't know, sir.'

Jowett pushed back his chair and stood up, to the sound of splintering glass. 'Let us not deceive ourselves, Sergeant. I spoke to you before of our concern at the knowledge the dynamite party appears to have of our methods. You remember the matter of the reliefs at the railway stations? We now appear to face an enemy which has got to know the very room in which the campaign against it is being mounted. Which passes freely into Scotland Yard to deposit an infernal machine in a convenience under our very – er—'

'Noses, sir?'

'Noses. And walks away without anyone noticing a thing. Doesn't that tend to confirm that the Clan-na-Gael is as knowledgeable about police matters as you or I or the Commissioner himself?'

'I'm afraid it does, sir.'

'At least we understand each other. Now, if you will come with me, I shall show you the other discovery of which I spoke.'

Jowett lifted his bowler hat from the stand, blew off a layer of dust, and led Cribb out of his office and downstairs. In the Yard outside, they negotiated the debris and made their way to a grille situated at the foot of a wall, out of view of the crowd. A black bag was resting on it.

'We put it where it could cause the least damage,' Jowett explained. 'No one here knew whether it was liable to explode, you understand. However, Colonel Martin himself came out to see it during the night and he has pronounced it harmless. You may examine it if you wish.'

Cribb crouched beside the bomb – for the charred end of a fuse protruding from the bag left no doubt of its identity. He felt inside and took out a piece of brass tubing, into which the other end of the fuse was inserted, and secured by a nipper. Fortunately the fuse had gone out before the flame reached the fulminate. He felt the bag's weight. Six or seven pounds, he estimated – quite enough to reduce a sizeable building to rubble. He tipped the dynamite out on the ground at his feet. From the corner of his eye, he noticed Jowett's shoes take a long step backwards. Without looking round, he picked up one of the cakes of dynamite and examined it. Atlas Powder: a standard six-ounce disc.

'It looks as though the dynamiters have given up the clockwork method of detonation, sir,' he told the Inspector, who remained just within earshot. 'Fuses may be dangerous to use, but they're clearly more successful. I wonder what stopped this one from working.'

'A small boy, if my information is correct,' said Jowett. 'He saw the thing smouldering and stamped it out with the heel of his boot, resourceful lad. Then he drew it to the attention of a constable on duty in the Square.'

'The Square? Which square was that, sir?'

'Trafalgar, no less. The bomb was quietly fizzing at the foot of Nelson's Column, beside the Landseer lion that looks towards St Martin's. These people will stop at nothing, Cribb. Nelson's Column – imagine!'

Cribb declined to imagine. It would take more than seven pounds of Atlas Powder to shift Nelson from his perch. The lion might have looked a little the worse for the experience, he was ready to admit.

'The prospect leaves me speechless, too,' Jowett went on. 'Would you believe that the constable who found the thing brought it over from Trafalgar Square in a hansom? When he arrived I was engaged in conversation with Inspector Littlechild, of the Special Branch, assessing the damage to the *Rising Sun* over a glass of porter that the landlord had most civilly provided. The devastation around us weighed heavily on our minds, Cribb, for when the fellow stumbled in carrying the black bag and muttering something about an infernal machine, we moved as one – straight behind the counter on our knees with the barman. It is a long time since I was constrained to do anything so undignified. After a minute's precautionary interval, we prevailed upon the constable by signals to convey the bag out of the *Rising Sun* and deposit it on the grille here. We were not in a position to know that the bomb was no longer active, you appreciate.'

Cribb stood up. Jowett's self-justifying held no interest for him. It was time the conversation changed. 'What's your reason for bringing me here, sir?'

'Eh?' The directness of the question – coming as it did from a mere detective-sergeant – produced the effect on Jowett that infernal machines did. He took a step backwards.

Cribb leaned towards him. 'I appreciate the gravity of the situation, sir, and I can see that what has happened here has a certain bearing on what we talked about three weeks ago, before I was sent to Woolwich. But if you've had Colonel Martin, the Inspector of Explosives, here, what's the purpose of sending for me? Three weeks don't count for much in experience of bombs, sir.'

'Granted. That is all you are going to get, however,' said Jowett, recovering his poise. 'You will not be returning to the Arsenal. Your services are otherwise required. It is manifestly clear, is it not, that the Clan-na-Gael must have been in possession of privileged information to carry out last night's detestable work?'

'Looks like that, sir.'

'And who do you suppose provided them with such information?'

'I can't imagine, sir,' said Cribb. It was not strictly true. A possibility had stirred in his brain the moment he saw the devastation in the Yard.

'Can't you? I can. I am not so confoundedly sentimental. You know as well as I which member of the C.I.D. has been drinking with Irish-Americans.'

40

'That was weeks ago, sir.'

'Do you suppose we have not been following his move-ments ever since? Constable Bottle of the Special Branch was assigned to that duty before you left Woolwich – a first-rate man, I might add. We set him up in rooms in Paradise Street, so that he was able to maintain a continuous vigil. He gave us a comprehensive written report on your encounter with Thackeray at London Bridge – and after-wards in *The Feathers*.'

'Waste of paper,' said Cribb. 'If you'd asked me, I'd have told you all you wanted to know, sir.'

'Possibly,' said Jowett, without much conviction. 'That is of small account now, however. I think you should know, Cribb, that when I arrived here in the early hours of this morning and took in this unbelievable scene, my first action was to send a telegraph to Bottle, demanding an immediate account of Thackeray's movements in the last forty-eight hours. The message was not delivered because Bottle was out of his rooms.'

'At that time, sir?'

'My own reaction exactly. I therefore sent a second message to Paradise Street police station to establish the whereabouts of Constable Thackeray. I was informed by return message that he was absent without permission, having failed to report for the midnight roll-call in the section-house. The news did not surprise me. It matched the information about Bottle. It was reasonable to assume that Thackeray's disappearance was not unconnected with the outrages here and in St James's Square, and that Bottle was on his trail.'

Jowett paused. Cribb waited expressionlessly.

'In that, I was mistaken. A message arrived from Thames

Division shortly after four o'clock. A body was taken from the river in the early hours of this morning in Limehouse Reach. Special Branch have already identified it as Bottle. A bullet had penetrated his brain.'

4

That same afternoon found Cribb marching purpose-fully out of West Brompton station and along Seagrave Road in the direction of Lillie Bridge, the metropolitan venue of athletic sports and bicycle-racing. Some fifty yards along, he took out his watch, checked the time, and turned left into a public house. As he had anticipated, the bar was thick with customers, many dressed as he was, in morning suit and black silk hat. He took his tankard and settled inconspicuously at a table near the skittle-alley. Four men in shirt sleeves and striped trousers were engrossed in a game, one, he noted with satisfaction, similar in build to himself.

He sipped his beer. The sequence of deductions that had brought him here had required an agonizing effort of concentration. Secretly, he envied the easy, irresistible logic of sixpenny-novel detectives, and would have liked to employ it in his own investigations. But now that Thackeray had disappeared, he was hard put to it to summon two consecutive thoughts. Irregular as their association over the past five years had been, slight as the confidences were that they had exchanged, the two of them had achieved an understanding that ran deep. When Jowett had blandly assumed Thackeray had some part in the bombing of

Scotland Yard – his second home – Cribb's anger had risen like the head on the beer. It had sunk at the news of the disappearance; dispersed altogether when he learned of Constable Bottle's death.

At length, he had decided to introduce some discipline into his thinking by making a list of the particulars Thackeray had given him about the Irish-American customers at *The Feathers*. Most notably, the man Malone. It was a curious vignette: a 'barge-horse of a man' over six feet in height, with manicured fingernails and calloused palms smelling of methylated spirit. Generous with his money, too; you had to be, to buy rounds of whisky at ninepence a tot. What was a rich American doing getting his hands blistered like that? A manual occupation could safely be discounted. Regular work with the hands would have hardened the skin beyond the stage of blistering. This was surely the purpose of the methylated spirit: to toughen soft skin in readiness for unaccustomed use, a precaution widely employed by amateur oarsmen. Could the muscular Mr Malone be a sportsman then, the stroke, perhaps, of some all-conquering American university crew bound for Henley? In plain truth it seemed unlikely. The training of American crews was reputed to be so rigorous that any Yankee oarsman must have developed palms like boot-soles before coming to England. No, if Malone practised manly exercises at all – and, confound it, there was *something* familiar about his name – it had to be a less demanding pastime. Punting? Pulling on a punt-pole certainly produced blisters, but it hardly seemed an adequate occupation for a human barge-horse. He had to think of a sport that employed a generous physique in a manly fashion, yet could be indulged in so occasionally that blistered hands resulted.

It was, of course, throwing the hammer. Cribb reached this confident conclusion by way of basketball, cricket, hockey and hurling. The last was an engaging possibility, except that to his knowledge not a single hurley had been put to use on the English side of the Irish Channel. It did, however, direct his thoughts to sports with strong Gaelic associations, of which hammer-throwing most emphatically suggested itself. All observant readers of the sporting press knew that Irish-Americans were as dextrous with sixteen-pound hammers as Englishmen with umbrellas.

A visit to the *Referee* offices in Fleet Street to study the files had provided the confirmation Cribb wanted, a series of references in the column *Athletic Intelligence*, beginning in February. 'The four members of the Gaelic American Athletic Club presently visiting this country,' said the most recent,

are expected to attract a large concourse to Lillie Bridge on Saturday next, when they appear in the London Athletic Club sports. If their appearances to date have not been marked by the universal success which has attended American visitors in previous seasons, the public will have noted that they have been rounding into form of late and may be expected to give a good account of themselves on Saturday. Creed, the hundred yards man, we are reliably informed has clocked 10 seconds several times in training recently, and on this form is unlikely to be troubled by Wood and Cowie, the pick of the home runners. In the high jump, P. Shanahan may have to repeat his leap of 5 feet 11 inches at Croydon last week to defeat Colbourne, the Inter Varsity Champion. Of the two

American hammer-throwers, Devlin looks the likelier to win again, although T. P. Malone, a veritable Goliath in stature, threatens to project the implement out of the ground and into Lillie Road if he can but master the trick of turning in the circle.

A shout from the end of the skittle-alley heralded an interesting throw. Seven of the nine pins had fallen. Cribb watched as the player retrieved the 'cheese' and returned to the mark to aim at the remaining skittles. It wanted considerable strength to dislodge so many, for they weighed seven pounds each. He was broadly-built and carried himself well for a man past fifty. An ex-athlete, Cribb decided. The second throw knocked aside the nearer of the standing pins, but altogether missed the other, on the extreme right of the diamond-shaped platform. By chance, however, the upended skittle made contact with another after it had left the platform and bounced back with just sufficient force to topple its mate.

'A single!' declared the thrower in triumph. 'Set 'em up for another throw, partner. I'll floor 'em this time.'

'Wait a moment, Holloway.' The man whose build resembled Cribb's put up a restraining hand.

'What's the matter? It's a bloody single. Nine pins down. I've got a chance for the double.'

'Eight down, old fellow. The last one doesn't count.'

'What do you mean, doesn't count? It was a fair lob.'

'Fair lob,' repeated the thrower's partner, a small man in his sixties, who was better at standing the skittles up than knocking them down.

'The lob was fair, yes, but it only accounted for one of the pins. The other doesn't count.'

'It *does*, Carter,' said the big man, petulantly. 'The first pin rebounded on to the platform and knocked the other bugger off.'

Cribb got to his feet. 'Possibly I can render some assistance, gentleman, as a detached observer, who knows something about the game. That is, if you would like an adjudicator.'

'Most civil of you,' said Carter thankfully. 'What do you say, gentlemen?'

Holloway and his partner exchanged dubious glances.

'For Heaven's sake! This afternoon we're timekeepers and judges ourselves,' said Carter. 'Surely we are willing to submit to the decisions of a referee in our own competition?'

Cribb was appointed by a consensus of nods and mutterings.

'And we'll stand you a drink at the end,' Carter bounteously suggested. 'Now, sir. We await your arbitration over the matter of the last throw. Were both pins fairly knocked down, in your judgement, or was there an infringement of the regulations?'

Holloway stood hugely among the fallen skittles with his thumbs hitched in his waistcoat, awaiting the verdict. Everyone looked expectantly towards Cribb.

A contingency he was quite prepared for. 'Before I settle the question, gentlemen, I must ask you, as your referee, whose set of rules you favour, Cassell's or Bohn's. On Cassell's authority, the final knockdown would be regarded as a foul, whereas Bohn would undeniably allow it. In the circumstances,' he went on, without pause, 'I propose that you commence a fresh game under my authority. The rules are as practised in the *Ratcatcher* in Victoria Street, namely three

47

sets of three throws for each player, no follow-throughs across the line, all knockdowns to count, except those perpetrated by a cheese or skittle after it has left the frame, and all the pins to be reset if anyone succeeds in flooring them with his first or second lob.'

To have continued arguing about the last skittle after such a categorical exposition of the rules would have done no credit to anyone. Honour satisfied, the game commenced in earnest, Cribb first casually removing his morning-coat and hooking it on the hatstand next to the one he had already marked as Carter's. Things were happening as well as he could wish.

Victory went to Holloway and his partner by 42 points to 37. 'Time for another game?' asked Cribb, as he wiped the blackboard clear. 'You're officiating at the sports this afternoon like me, I gather. When do we report, do you remember?'

'By ten minutes past two,' said Carter, consulting his watch. 'Yes, there's time. Set them up, Holloway, and I'll fetch a drink for our referee. We're on beer, sir. Will that do? We're all still drinking, I take it?' He moved to the bar.

'Damned chalk,' Cribb remarked to Holloway's partner. 'Gets all over your clothes if you ain't careful.' He showed him a set of dusty fingers and crossed towards the hatstand. There, he sedulously smeared chalk around his jacket pocket as he felt for a handkerchief with his right hand. His left, still scrupulously free of dust, simultaneously transplanted a large rosette with the word *Official* on it from Carter's lapel to his own.

He returned to the blackboard, rubbing both hands with his handkerchief. Carter arrived with a tray of drinks, and the skittles restarted. This time the result was reversed.

Holloway's partner was quite unable any longer to pitch with sufficient force to disturb the pins.

'That's it, gentlemen,' Cribb announced. 'Thirty-eight points wins. All square, and no time for a decider. We shall have to be reporting.' He walked to the hatstand and removed the jacket with the rosette. 'Yours, I think, Mr Carter.'

Carter put it on and immediately sensed something wrong. He patted the pockets and looked at the lining. 'I don't think it is mine. Look, here's some chalkmarks by the pocket. Must be yours, sir.'

'I do believe it is,' said Cribb, waiting in his shirtsleeves. 'That must be yours on the peg, then. I thought you said you were an official. Don't you have a rosette like the rest of us?'

Ten minutes after, he was marching across the centre of the Lillie Bridge arena, Carter's rosette still prominently displayed on his chest. Any stirrings of conscience he may have had about the acquisition were stilled by the certainty that Carter *sans* rosette would gain admission to the ground. They had all promised to stand by the poor fellow at the entrance for officials and competitors, before Cribb had felt obliged to go on ahead, since he was sure to be required for the hammer-throw. As he pointed out, it was always the first event on the programme.

For a mecca of healthful competition, Lillie Bridge was oddly situated, wedged between a railway marshalling yard and a fever hospital. The turf itself was overlain with a thin coat of soot. The track, of black cinders, and the several hundred silent, dark-suited, bowler-hatted spectators on the terracing, completed a distinctly sombre panorama. A hearse would not have looked out of place there.

The hammer-circle, in the interests of public safety, was sited on the side of the ground farthest from the stand where the spectators were gathered. The arrangement suited Cribb. Three hammer-throwers were flexing themselves nearby, but for the present he concentrated on the two officials standing by the circle in conversation. Their reception of him was critical to the outcome of the afternoon.

They turned on hearing his approach, both barrel-shaped figures of no great height, with decidedly bad-tempered expressions on their faces. He was reminded of Tweedledum and Tweedledee.

'What part do you propose to play in this pantomime?' said the first.

'This *is* the hammer throw, is it not?' said Cribb. The safest answer to a question like that was another question.

'If it isn't, this is a damned peculiar place to stand every Saturday,' said the second. 'I don't know why you're here. The two of us have managed tolerably well for the past three seasons without assistance.'

Regulars – what wretched luck! On an inspiration Cribb answered, 'It must be on account of our Transatlantic Cousins. They have difficulty in understanding our rules for hammer-throwing, I believe.'

'So do I, by George,' said the first. 'The rules are changing all the time. Wasn't more than four years ago we allowed 'em unlimited runs. They started over there somewhere and came spinning past here like teetotums. It was in the lap of the gods which got thrown farther, the hammer or the man. More than one of the crowd got picked off by badly aimed hammers, too. Serve 'em right – they only came to watch because it was comical. You don't get that class of person now that it's all done from seven-foot circles. There's still an element of danger, mind. Where did you intend to stand?'

'I thought I might make myself useful by retrieving the hammers,' said Cribb. That would put him in the front line, but it promised to be less suicidal than standing by the circle to check the movements of the throwers' feet.

'Very well. Keep your wits about you, though. This isn't cricket, you know. There's no credit given for catching them before they land.'

Cribb formed his mouth into the token of a smile and started watchfully along the margin of the throwing area. He was determined not to take his eyes off the hammer-circle so long as he was within range. The throwers were practising their turns, keeping a firm grip on their hammers and rotating like whirling dervishes.

He took up a stance on the bicycle track, in line with the second official, who positioned himself rashly in the very centre of the arena. Presently there was a shrill whistle-blast from the first, a vigorous brandishing of a Union Jack, and one of the throwers stepped into the circle, spat into the palm of each hand, swung the hammer several times through an axis above his head, brought it lower, turned his body with it and let go.

It thudded into the turf some thirty feet from Cribb. The second official hurried towards it and marked the spot with an iron pin with a pennant attached. Cribb took hold of the wooden shaft of the hammer and disinterred the metal head by a series of jerks. The movement dislodged his silk hat and sent it careering across the grass. 'For Heaven's sake,' said the second official as he returned it to him, 'let's endeavour to preserve a modicum of dignity,

51

old fellow. There's enough antics going on at the other end, without you and me setting up in opposition.'

In their present situation, it was courting disaster to prolong conversation further, so he picked up the hammer and stumbled to the sideline without a word. There, he started the walk back towards the circle, dragging the implement behind him like a sledge, for exhibitions of strength were no more suitable from officials than antics with hats.

He was met halfway by the thrower, a generously-built fellow, not quite a barge-horse, but impressive enough about the flanks and withers. 'I'll need to turn faster than that to bother the Yankees,' he confided to Cribb in the unconfidential accents of the English upper class. 'I fancy that this hammer is a trifle short in the shaft. See if you can get hold of Devlin's and pass it on to me, there's a good chap. I'll wait here.'

There was nothing against it in the rules he had thought-fully consulted that morning, so he nodded and made for the centre of the field, where the second hammer had already embedded itself, some ten feet past the Englishman's mark. When it was marked, he wrenched it from the turf and hauled it over to the waiting athlete.

'Stout fellow!' said the Englishman. He grabbed the handle and made off towards the circle at some speed, taking care not to catch the eye of the American fast approaching Cribb.

'Where's m'hammer?' demanded the new arrival. He was the shorter of the foreign opposition, a mere six feet or so of shaggy Irish-American muscularity. This must be Devlin, Cribb decided. It wouldn't do to anger him.

Cribb winked theatrically. 'I think you'll find there's more whip on this one. This shaft is made of malacca, you see. The other's hickory. I passed it to the Englishman.' He winked again, in case the first had not been noticed.

Devlin frowned, and examined the hammer-handle dubiously. 'Now why should you do a thing like that?'

Cribb shrugged. 'Maybe there's a drop of Erin blood in my veins.'

'Ah!' Devlin seemed to understand. He winked at Cribb and walked away, dangling the hammer like a toy.

During this conversation, the third hammer had been launched and had landed several yards short of the previous throws. Cribb retrieved it and towed it to the side of the throwing area. In his keenness to get clear before the whistle blew again, he practically butted his silk hat into the midriff of the third competitor.

Malone did not budge an inch. If Cribb's forward motion had not been independently halted at the last possible instant, there is no question that the injuries would have been all on his side. 'I do apologize,' he said.

Malone put forward a massive hand for his hammer. The sections of his limbs not covered by the black merino of guernsey and drawers supported a growth of hair so abundant that it would not have wanted much imagination to believe him clothed from head to toe in black. When Cribb looked up into the two small eyes that, together with a once-fractured nose, were all that could be seen of Malone's face behind a mass of glossy curls, he had the curious fancy that they were regarding him from the centre of a heap of blackberries. It was not a fruit he liked.

Malone took the hammer without a word and strode away. Cribb studied his vast, retreating figure. It was baffling that a man of those proportions could not hurl a sixteen pound weight farther than lesser mortals like Devlin and the Englishman. Possibly Malone was equally baffled.

The next throw from the Englishman drifted well off centre, but it was a long one that took him into the lead. 'It's a little beauty!' he told Cribb, when he collected the hammer. 'Let's see if Uncle Sam can match that!'

Devlin's throw, unhappily, was ten feet behind his first effort. Cribb discerned unmistakable aggression in the set of the Irish-American's shoulders as he came forward for the malacca-handled hammer. 'Did you see that throw of mine? I think you handed me a bum hammer, Mister. Are you sure about that Irish blood of yours?'

'As sure as I am that you'll beat him with your last throw,' said Cribb, with all the passion he could raise. 'I think you gave it too much height, if I might proffer an opinion. The shaft is giving you the extra whip. You have my word for that.'

'D'you really think so?' said Devlin, prepared to be convinced.

'I had the very devil of a job pulling it out of the turf,' said Cribb. 'There's power in that malacca, I promise you.'

'There has to be. I shall need over a hundred feet to win this afternoon.'

At the other end, Malone was in the circle. His efforts with the hammer aped the style of the other competitors without achieving the same fluidity. Instead of swinging the hammerhead through a series of circles in a gradually accelerating movement, he somehow contrived to begin like a fly-wheel at full speed and end like a novice with a yo-yo. On sheer arm-power the hammer swung aloft and dropped like a plummet not twenty yards from the circle. Cribb decided it was prudent to let him collect the implement himself.

The Englishman's third throw was no longer than his second, so it was open to the Americans to clinch the contest with their final efforts. For once in his life, Cribb gritted his teeth and hoped Britannia would not prevail. There were bigger things at issue than victory in a sporting competition. The winning of Devlin's confidence was more important for England this afternoon.

The lead weight at the end of the malacca handle flashed in the sun as it was pulled through its preliminary orbits. Three times it passed above Devlin's head before he allowed his body to contribute to the momentum, turning with the hammer, spinning with singular agility on the balls of his feet. Then at the moment of maximum acceleration, his right leg stiffened at the front edge of the circle and he released the hammer. It described a great arc above the blackness of Lillie Bridge and shuddered down in the centre of the throwing-sector.

From where Cribb stood, the throw looked at least the equal of the Englishman's. With the greatest difficulty, he resisted the impulse to cheer. He ran to the mark to make quite sure he was not deceived by some trick of perspective. 'It's a long one,' said the second official superfluously. 'There won't be much in it between the two of them. Did he put his foot out of the circle, do you suppose?'

The arrival of the first official from the opposite end led Cribb to wonder momentarily if such a calamity had taken place. Fortunately, it was not so. 'Mr Malone has elected not to take his last throw,' came the explanation, 'so we may now commence the measuring of the best effort of each competitor.' The second official took the end of the measuring-tape from his colleague with the familiarity of a well-established ritual and walked to the circle, pulling for more tape as he required it. Soon a quivering line was established between the front of the circle and Devlin's mark. 'One hundred and eight feet precisely,' announced the second official.

'Holy Mother of God!' exclaimed Devlin. 'I've never thrown anything so far in all my life. That's the sweetest little hammer I've ever held in my two hands.'

'Malacca,' Cribb reminded him, in an aside.

'Ah! Malacca.' Devlin winked.

The measuring-party moved tensely across to the Englishman's pennant at the extreme edge of the sector. At the front edge of the circle, the first official held his end of the tape rigidly in place. The second official was on his knees by the pin with everyone else clustered around him. The Englishman was the first to leap up in excitement. 'One hundred and eight feet one, by Heaven! I've done it by an inch.' He snatched Devlin's hand and shook it vigorously. 'Splendid competition, old man. You certainly brought out the best in me. You too.' He nodded in Malone's direction, but did not go so far as to shake his hand.

'That's it, then. Congratulations,' said Devlin.

'Just a moment.' The voice was Cribb's. He was standing at the circle, beside the first official. 'I should like the throw to be measured again according to the rules,' he called. 'I think we may find a discrepancy.'

The Englishman strode the thirty-five yards to where Cribb was standing. 'Just what do you intend by that remark, sir?'

'That we are subject to the regulations of the Amateur Athletic Association,' said Cribb mildly. 'If I may quote – and I think I can – "All distances shall be measured from the circumference of the circle to the first pitch of the hammer, *along a line drawn from that pitch to the centre of the circle.*" The latter was not observed in this case, gentlemen. The measuring of both throws was taken from the same spot at the front of the circle. It would not, of course, affect the measuring of Mr Devlin's throw, which happened to be in line with the front, but I suggest that we re-measure the other.'

'I believe he's right,' conceded the first official. 'The bloody laws are always being changed.'

'Not this one,' said Cribb. 'It has been in force for several years.'

The tape was extended again, this time between the Englishman's mark and the point of the circle nearest to it.

'One hundred and seven feet, eleven and a half inches,' said the second official. 'Mr Devlin wins.'

'You're a son of Erin, by Jesus!' said a voice in Cribb's ear.

5

'This is most civil of you,' said Cribb, indicating the pint of ale in front of him.

'Not at all,' said Devlin. 'It's a poor sort of man that doesn't repay a kindness. I don't let opportunities like this slip by.'

Nor I, thought Cribb. He had not gone to so much trouble merely for a glass of beer. 'I was doing my job, no more. It was simply a matter of exercising the rules.'

'That may be so,' said Devlin, 'but 'twould have been easier to have held your tongue. The sport could do with more of your kind, mister – men of principle, that take their duties seriously. Incidentally, you're not wanted for the high jump, or anything, are you?'

'Lord, no.' Cribb shook his head decisively and transferred the official rosette slickly into his pocket. 'We tend to specialize in one event, you know.' He smiled. 'The rules get more complicated all the time.'

'Sure, and don't you think I know that? It's taken me a year and more to master the art of turning in a pesky little seven-foot circle.'

What an opening! Cribb took a sip of beer and casually said, 'It's an art your friend Mr Malone doesn't appear to have mastered yet.'

Devlin returned a sharp look. 'Malone? Malone's no friend of mine.'

'Indeed?' said Cribb. 'I apologize for the error.' As Devlin showed no sign of wanting to enlarge on his statement, the sergeant went on. 'I had assumed you were constantly competing together. In England, the principal hammer-throwers comprise a very – if you'll pardon the expression – small circle.'

The reference made no impression on Devlin. He stared absently into his beer.

'And then again,' said Cribb, determined not to drop the subject, 'I should have thought you would have got to know each other tolerably well on the voyage from America. I presume you were all on the same Cunarder.'

'Sure,' said Devlin, 'but Malone was travelling on his own ticket like a gentleman. The rest of us were steerage. The first time I spoke to him was after we had docked at Southampton.' He emphasized his words in a way clearly intended to remove any question of his involvement with Malone.

But if *that* line of inquiry was closed, another was now open. 'He is somewhat detached from the other members of the team, then?' said Cribb.

'That's about it,' said Devlin, relieved that the point was taken at last.

'He isn't quartered with the rest of you, I dare say?'

Devlin shook his head. 'He's taken a suite in some flash hotel in Piccadilly – the Alcazar. The rest of us are dossing down in something not much better than a common lodging-house here in West Brompton. It's convenient for Lillie Bridge, but there the convenience ends.'

'I'm sorry to hear that,' said Cribb.

'Ah, we wouldn't really want to be in a hotel. We're not accustomed to it. Shanahan and I are at college, you see, and Creed works in a druggist's store. We're all dependent on the club for our upkeep here.'

'Not so Malone?' said Cribb.

'Not so Malone.'

'He is a man of private means, then?'

'I think you could say that.'

'I follow you now,' said Cribb, as if Devlin had been struggling all afternoon to make himself clear. 'If a man is a passable athlete and can pay his way, the club will allow him to wear its colours. Ah well, it may seem unjust that a man can buy himself a place on an international team, but after all, the same thing happens in every other sphere of human activity, Mr Devlin, and I daresay there are less wholesome things to be bought with money than athletic club vests. The exercise Mr Malone is getting must be most beneficial. Perhaps he will blossom into a champion by the time you all return. He's got the physical capacity, wouldn't you say?'

'He's a big fellow, I'll grant you,' Devlin conceded, 'but he'll need to learn the rudiments of turning in the circle before anyone can call him a hammer-thrower.'

'That was evident this afternoon,' Cribb agreed. 'But surely he will improve with practise? I cannot believe that a man so enthusiastic about his athletics as to cross the ocean for competition is not taking the most elementary steps to improve his style.'

'Believe what you like,' said Devlin. 'You saw him this afternoon. He's been here since February.'

'Really? How very odd!' said Cribb, pleased at the way the conversation flowed more freely now it was concerned with the demands of hammer-throwing. 'If the man doesn't practise, how on earth does he keep himself in condition? Does he have a set of bar-bells at the Alcazar Hotel, do you think?'

'If you want to know, I reckon he's more accustomed to lowering pints than lifting weights,' said Devlin. 'The only exercise he gets is in the contest when he represents the club. He gets by on sheer size and brute strength. He knows he's less than fit, too. That's the reason why he entered for the shot-putting as well as the hammer this afternoon – to shake some of the lead out of his limbs.'

Cribb nodded. The last assumption was probably true. If Malone's training for athletics was restricted to Saturday afternoons, he would want to take all the opportunities of exercise that the programme of events offered. Of far more interest was what kept him from practising at other times, what had brought him from America – for it was evidently not hammer-throwing.

'He's a drinking man, you say? That's unusual in an athlete, isn't it? I've heard of pugilists sneaking into public houses or carrying their little bottles of liquor about with 'em, but I thought you amateurs trained upon temperance principles.'

Devlin grinned. 'You don't know much about the Gaelic American Athletic Club, then. We're none of us averse to a drop of the hard stuff once in a while – and what do you think we use for embrocation?'

'He can't possibly spend all his time at the bar,' persisted Cribb.

'I've never thought it part of my business to ask him.'

There was enough rebuke in the answer to show Cribb that he would not get any further. Whatever Devlin privately thought Malone was doing on the other six days of the week, he was not going to be drawn into discussing it that afternoon. The sergeant got to his feet. 'Ah well, it takes all sorts to make an athletics team, eh, Mr Devlin? I think I'll amble back to the ground now and see how things are progressing. What time is the shot-putting expected to start?'

'Four o'clock, I believe.'

'It's almost that already. I wonder whether Mr Malone will fare any better without a bar attached to the weight than with one.'

As it happened, Cribb had no intention of finding out. After looking in briefly at Lillie Bridge and satisfying himself that Malone was still there (in fact, limbering up conscientiously for his event), he hailed the first hansom cab that passed along Seagrave Road and told the driver to take him to the Alcazar Hotel in Arundel Place.

The streets of Brompton basked in the sunshine which had finally broken through, their Saturday afternoon somnolence altogether remote from dynamite and death. As Cribb watched the parasol parade from his cab, the smell of tar from the joints of the Earls Court Road's wooden pavement was wafted through carriage-dust to his nostrils. Memories of perambulations in winsome company on summer afternoons drifted across his mind, until the sight of a blue helmet jerked him back to his present commission. He trained his thoughts on Constable Bottle and his ignominious end, and pressed himself farther back against the leather upholstery. It was not impossible that the Clan already had him under scrutiny; his doings at Lillie Bridge had been a calculated risk. What if Malone had not been taken in by the top hat and official rosette? The dangers in this business were extreme, and all the more unnerving for being played out in such unlikely spots as railway stations and sporting arenas. In all truth he would have felt more comfortable face to face with his enemy in some ill-lit back room of an Irish public house.

Arundel Place, one of those odd little culs-de-sac within a few yards of Piccadilly Circus, yet quite detached from the hub of the Empire, was approached from Coventry Street. It was well-known to the Vine Street police – on whose strength Cribb had served in his time – as a peculiarly rewarding point of duty. Lambert's, the silversmith's on the corner, paid the Force thirty shillings a week to have a constable on night watch outside, and in return for keeping his eyes open (or closed, according to circumstances) the fortunate officer could make almost that amount in tips from the distinguished residents of the Georgian houses and three hotels that comprised the street. At the end, it broadened into a small square, in which the Alcazar Hotel was prominent, its Georgian portico projecting on to the pavement, with twin potted ferns at each side of the open front door.

Cribb paid the cabman and climbed three carpeted steps to the hotel foyer. It was ten years at least since he had last been there, at the night-porter's invitation, for a glass of something warm in the small hours of a January morning. He was half-prepared to be recognized, for hotel staff have long memories, but he retained a hope that the silk hat and morning suit were sufficiently unsuggestive of helmet and great-coat to preserve his incognito. It chanced that no one was present when he entered, and after a short appraisal of *The Bath of Psyche* over the mantelpiece, he settled on a sofa to wait. Without knowing the location of

Malone's room, he did not propose to wander aimlessly about the hotel. Nor was he moved to make a rapid examination of the register lying open on the reception-desk; unless there were over-riding disadvantages in the procedure, he preferred to conduct his inquiries in a civilized fashion.

Just as well, for the receptionist appeared rapidly and without warning from a door behind the desk, a young woman with hair cut square over her brow and loosely knotted behind in the modern style. To his relief, Cribb had not seen her before.

'I do apologize, sir. You haven't been waiting long, I hope?'

'A few minutes, no more. I believe that you have a Mr Malone, from America, staying here. I was desirous of meeting him.'

'Mr Malone? Oh, yes – the sporting gentleman. I am not sure if he is in. He comes and goes rather, and doesn't always advise us of his movements. If you'll kindly wait a moment, sir, I'll arrange for a page to go up to his suite. Do you have a card, sir?'

A card! The topper and tails *were* making an impact. 'He doesn't know me by name,' Cribb explained. 'But if the boy would care to mention the Metropolitan Athletic Club . . .'

He made sure he was within earshot when the page reported, and heard the receptionist send him to room 206. He managed to look fittingly disappointed at the news, a few minutes later, that Mr Malone was not in his suite.

'You are welcome to wait, if you have the time,' the receptionist told him. 'There is a lounge to your left, and the smoking-room beyond.'

He nodded his gratitude and moved in to the lounge, a large pink and white room. It had a deserted, Saturday afternoon look. One elderly resident dozed by the window under a copy of the *Morning Post*. He ventured through into the smoking-room, all leather and mahogany, and quite uninhabited. A baize door to the right of the fireplace attracted his attention, more than likely an entrance used by servants. The chance of getting upstairs by this route was too good to forgo. He pushed through the door into a narrow, uncarpeted passage. Some fifteen yards ahead, where it turned to the right, was a spiral staircase. Voices were coming from somewhere, too indistinct for him to make out individual words, but apparent from the tone that two or more female domestics were exchanging confidences. With luck, they would be too occupied with their conversation to disturb him. He hoped so; morning-dress might be an advantage in an hotel foyer, but it was difficult to account for in the servants' quarters.

He reached the stairs and mounted as noiselessly as he could to the second floor, where he made his way along a passage similar to the one he had first come through, and found himself in a linen-room stacked with bedding. He listened at the door, and hearing nothing, pulled it open and stepped on to the carpet of the second-floor corridor, not without a flutter of self-congratulation. Perhaps, after all, there was a future to be had in the Secret Service.

The corridor was as deserted as the rest of the hotel. He stepped boldly along it, counting the numbers on the doors until he came to 206. To be quite sure it was locked, he tested the handle; a pity his training at Woolwich had not included the forcing of locks. Short of sitting down to wait outside the door for Malone's return, there was one other expedient left to him. It called for the kind of heroics he would normally have entrusted to Thackeray, but this afternoon he had to take the initiative himself. He walked to the end of the corridor, pushed up a window, and peered out.

Thirty feet below, a pigeon was crossing Arundel Place. From Cribb's position, its waddling progress looked awkward in the extreme. Strange how a change of perspective altered the appearance of everyday things . . . He looked left along the side of the building, on a level with the second floor. More pigeons were clustered there, perched proprietorially along a ledge projecting some nine inches from the wall. It provided exactly what he required: a means of reaching the window of suite 206.

He removed his jacket and placed it neatly out of sight with the silk hat behind the folds of the curtain. He folded his shirt sleeves and lowered himself from the window to the ledge without another glance downwards. He hoped anyone who chanced to see him would suppose him a window-cleaner or house-painter going about his lawful employment. The square was deserted, so far as he could tell. He flattened his palms against the wall and began to move sideways. The pigeons did not disdain to leave the ledge as his feet appeared among them, but contrived to find a way around the invading shoes, grumbling chestily at the inconvenience. A small stone was dislodged and he heard it hit the pavement below. He wondered whether anyone was down there by now, looking up at him. He thought of Malone, and pondered how long it took to complete a shot-putting contest. He began to move with more urgency.

The window of 206 was partially open, and easy to push

up far enough for him to climb inside. Secure again, he looked down into Arundel Place to satisfy himself that his manoeuvre had not been observed. The pigeon was still in sole occupation.

Devlin had been right when he said Malone lived in style. The bedroom in which Cribb found himself was half as large again as any hotel-room he had been in before. He felt the pile of the carpet respond to the weight of his feet as he got up from the window-sill and crossed to an enamelled ash tallboy. The drawers contained clothes – collars, shirts and undergarments – and nothing to interest Scotland Yard. He tried the wardrobe and found two suits and an overcoat. The pockets were empty except for handkerchiefs.

He crossed to the bathroom. The luxury extended there in a gleaming chrome and enamel hot water geyser and a flawless white galvanized bath, but Cribb's attention was claimed at once by a bottle on the shelf over the wash-basin. It contained a purple-coloured liquid. He removed the top and sniffed it: methylated spirit, without any doubt at all. He sniffed it again for pure relish – the virtual confirmation that Malone was the man Thackeray had met in *The Feathers* in Rotherhithe. And beside it on the shelf was a box containing an ivory-handled manicure-set.

There was one more room to examine: the sitting room. It bore more traces of its tenant than the others, a pile of copies of the *Irish Post* on a table beside a decanter of whisky; a number of books, including the *London Directory*; and a collection of sporting impedimenta – Indian clubs, chest-expanders, even two throwing-hammers – stacked in a corner of the room from which all furniture and ornaments had been cleared, evidently to provide a small gymnasium.

Cribb bent to examine one of the hammers, an item of personal luggage unlikely to be tolerated in less exclusive hotels, he thought, particularly when it belonged to a whisky-drinking Irishman. On picking it up, he was surprised to find it lighter in weight than the hammers he had handled at Lillie Bridge. There was half a stone difference, at least. As he turned it over thoughtfully in his hand, he noticed a join midway along the wooden handle. He twisted the two halves away from each other and felt them give, and unscrew. They were hollow. Inside, were four glass tubes he recognized at once as detonators. It might have been a throwing-hammer he was holding, but it was also an infernal machine. He did not need to prise open the head to know that it was stuffed with dynamite.

The moment when a man discovers that the object in his hands is a bomb is not the best to take him by surprise. It says much for Cribb's cool-headedness that he did not drop the 'hammer' altogether at the sound of the lock turning in the door of the room. He swung round, still reassembling the handle, prepared to point out that any shot that felled him would surely account for his attacker too, and watched the door open. A young girl, not more than fifteen years old, marched boldly in, carrying a pillow-case.

'Oops! I'm sorry, sir! Thought you was out. I'm only the chambermaid, wanting to turn back the sheet on your bed.'

Cribb nodded. 'You carry on, young lady. Don't mind me. Just taking my daily exercise. I was about to go out, anyway.'

She bobbed a small, blushing curtsey and scuttled through to the bedroom. Cribb replaced the hammer in its original position and moved just as quickly out of suite

206 and into the corridor. Stopping only to retrieve his hat and coat, he located the main staircase and passed rapidly downstairs, heartily relieved when he reached the bottom without meeting Malone coming up, but retaining sufficient presence of mind to raise his hat to the receptionist as he crossed the foyer. He had done it, by Heaven! Single-handed, he had run a dynamiter to earth within hours of being assigned to the case. Inspector Jowett was due for the surprise of his career!

He hailed a four-wheeler that had appeared in the square. 'Great Scotland Yard,' he told the cabman. 'Make haste, man. Important business. Double fare!'

He climbed inside, sat down and found that he was not alone. Devlin was sitting opposite him. There was a gun in his hand directed at Cribb's chest.

6

The windows on the right were covered. Devlin leaned forward and pulled down the blinds on the left without shifting gaze or aim from Cribb. A small rear window some six inches square admitted sufficient light for the two men to see each other, but it was impossible for Cribb to follow which direction the cab was taking without turning in his seat and craning for a view, a manoeuvre he decided in the circumstances not to attempt.

'Now, Mister,' said Devlin, as the cab began to move, 'I'll thank you to remove your jacket and waistcoat and put them on the seat here beside me. I shan't hesitate to shoot if you try anything irregular.'

Was there anything more irregular than disrobing in a public carriage? Cribb obeyed without comment, leaving his top hat conspicuously in position. He wanted there to be no misunderstanding of his movements. Devlin had the look of a man who was not bluffing; he checked the pockets of each surrendered garment with his left hand, but the gun in his right remained steady.

'I'll have your braces and boots as well,' he told Cribb. 'To discourage you from trying anything foolish.'

He got them.

'Now, Mister. I think certain explanations are due. When

you left me last you were going back to Lillie Bridge to watch the shot-putting. Instead, you took the first cab available to Malone's hotel and when you came out you were in a devil of a hurry to get to Great Scotland Yard. But first things first. What's your name?'

'Sargent.' It was the first time Cribb had resorted to a false identity, but he had more than once speculated on the possibility and decided this was the most convenient name to adopt. It had the advantage of being unlikely to catch him out in an unguarded moment.

'Well, Mr Sargent, it's time you accounted for your interest in Malone.'

'Might I first inquire where we are going?'

'Not Scotland Yard, anyway,' said Devlin. 'I'm taking you to meet somebody who'll be interested to hear about the goings-on at Lillie Bridge and Arundel Place this afternoon.'

'Mr Malone?'

'Somebody more important than that, Mr Sargent. Now, then!' He waved the gun in a menacing way. 'What do you want with Malone?'

This time, Cribb did not make the quick response expected of him. Without realizing it, Devlin had just forfeited the chance of extracting information from his prisoner. He had told Cribb the purpose of the journey, admitted the existence of a 'more important' person. This at once diminished his own status. Before, the threat he represented to Cribb was limitless; he might have been judge, jury and executioner himself. Now, he was revealed as a humble escort, whose first duty was to deliver the prisoner to his superior.

'I'll explain it all when we get there,' said Cribb, good-humouredly. There was nothing to be gained from baiting

71

Devlin. He would do what he could to keep the conversation on a civilized plane. 'There's a lot to tell, and I wouldn't want to have to repeat it all when we got there. Might miss something out the second time, and that wouldn't do, would it?'

Devlin frowned, unprepared for this development.

A siren sounded outside.

'Ah! Steamship on the right,' said Cribb. 'This must be the Embankment. Am I right? The surfaces of these new roads produce a most distinctive sound when carriage wheels pass over them, don't you agree? The Strand just now had quite a different resonance.'

Devlin had the uncomfortable look of one who had lost the initiative without understanding how. He gripped the gun until his knuckles whitened. 'Right turn, then,' said Cribb, so patently ridiculous in top hat, shirt sleeves and unsupported trousers that Devlin's capitulation appeared pathetic in the extreme. 'We're crossing Blackfriars Bridge. See if there isn't a whiff of whelks from the stalls on the other side.' As self-appointed guide, he launched into a commentary on the route, using whatever information reached his ears and nostrils. And there appeared to, be so many identifiable breweries, leather-markets and gasworks south of the Thames that Devlin might as well have put up the blinds and abandoned the pretence of a secret destination. As they crossed the wind-swept expanse of Blackheath, Cribb actually went so far as to suggest a halt. 'There's Shooter's Hill to come, and I'm beginning to fear for the health of the horse. These old hacks ain't used to ten mile journeys, you know. Even the buses change animals to get up Shooter's.'

Devlin's eyes had suddenly become redder and distinctly

narrower at the edges. 'Sargent, it ill-becomes an Irishman to stifle conversation, I know, but if you don't stop that bell-clapper of yours this minute I'll blow your bloody brains out.'

It seemed a strong response to a mild inquiry on behalf of a dumb animal, but Cribb judged it prudent not to pursue the point. There was quiet satisfaction a few minutes later when the driver made an unprompted stop.

'Don't attempt to open that door, Sargent,' Devlin warned.

A pained look appeared on Cribb's face. 'Dressed like this?'

They passed through Bexley and Dartford before the sameness of Watling Street was exchanged for a more winding route in the direction, Cribb estimated aloud, of Gravesend. Whether he was right he did not discover, for after three-quarters of a mile the carriage left the tar macadam for a cart-track. The jolting in consequence was not only extremely uncomfortable; in Cribb's position, it was downright dangerous. The trigger-mechanism of an American Smith and Wesson revolver, he kept assuring himself, required strong pressure from the finger. The things didn't *usually* fire involuntarily, but then they weren't usually handled by hammer-throwers in agitated carriages. The relief after this of moving on to a stretch of level gravel was so exquisite that when the carriage presently stopped, his hand went unthinkingly to the door-handle.

'Don't touch it!' Devlin almost screamed. 'Pick up your things and wait until you're told to move.'

He obeyed, wishing there were some way of conveying that he had not the slightest intention of escaping. Now that he had got over the shame of being taken by surprise in Arundel Place, he could see advantages in his situation. It was uncommonly decent of the dynamiters to have arranged a cab for him. Goodness knows how long it would have taken otherwise to locate their headquarters. He needed only to keep his nerve, give a plausible account of himself, and the secrets of the dynamite conspiracy were there for the taking – among them, of course, the mystery of Thackeray's disappearance. Indeed, the only points of outstanding concern to him were those on which he would shortly have to put his stockinged feet; but even that anxiety proved to be short-lived, for the cab unexpectedly began to move again, and he shortly felt the wheels move off the gravel on to a smoother surface, and stop.

Devlin let up one of the blinds to reveal a darling, white-washed wall. He kept the gun trained on Cribb, and felt for the cord on the other side. The blind went up with a disquieting snap. Cribb glanced outside. They were drawn up alongside a gig, in what appeared to be a coach-house of considerable size. 'Open the door and get out,' Devlin ordered. 'And go carefully, Mr Sargent. The gun will be pointing at the middle of your back.'

Cribb turned the handle and pushed open the door. With one hand gripping the waist-band of his trousers and the other supporting his bundle of clothes, he stooped to descend from the carriage without dislodging his hat, a singularly difficult manoeuvre.

'I'll render some assistance,' Devlin's voice volunteered from behind him. He felt the silk hat lifted gently from his head, followed at once by a staggering impact on the back of his skull. He pitched forward like a felled tree. There was no shock of pain, no frantic reaching out with the hands to break the fall. His one immediate reaction was to conclude – with extraordinary clarity and conviction – that he had not convinced Devlin of his willingness to co-operate. Damned unfortunate, that. He hit the ground and lay still.

The pain soon took over, the sensation of a clamp tightening turn by turn on his skull, a soreness in his left shoulder, which had struck the ground first, and a throbbing in his side, where Devlin had savagely kicked him after he fell. Instinctively he remained immobile, feigning loss of consciousness. More than once, as a young constable, he had been compelled to use this stratagem in public brawls; the secret of a long career in the Force was recognizing the moment when to retire from hostilities, and knowing how.

He heard Devlin talking to the driver, instructing him to unstrap the horse and water it. The man and his four-wheeler were evidently installed here at the disposal of the dynamiters. Devlin, presumably, had been driven to Lillie Bridge for the hammer-throwing, and had decided after his conversation with Cribb to drive round to Arundel Place. The carriage had looked like any other growler plying for hire in London's streets – which was perhaps convenient if you were interested in depositing infernal machines about the metropolis.

The sound of the horse's hooves receded. Devlin's footsteps approached to within a yard of Cribb. Lying there under inspection, not knowing whether to expect a bullet or another brutal kick, tested his self-discipline to the limit. He heard the movement of cloth close to his ear and knew Devlin was crouching for a closer examination. Under his closed eyelids he rotated his eyeballs upwards, a sensible precaution, for within seconds he felt a thumb on the right lid, pulling it up to check the state of insensibility. This must have satisfied Devlin, for he stood upright again and walked across the coach-house.

Cribb fractionally opened his eyes and watched his captor select a length of rope from several, coiled and suspended on nails in the wall. So Devlin had decided to tie him up. It would be interesting to see how he managed *that* with a gun in his hand.

The footsteps returned. Cribb took stock of himself, his head still singing from the blow that had floored him. It must have been the butt of the Smith and Wesson that Devlin had used, though it had felt like one of his throwing-hammers. The pains in his shoulder and side had eased somewhat. It was difficult to be sure, but things felt bruised rather than broken. If the chance he was waiting for materialized, he would assuredly take it.

Devlin reached him, stood pensively over him for a second or two, and then squatted by his feet and passed the rope underneath them, the revolver still in his right hand. Cribb watched this through a triangle formed by the underside of his right forearm, his chest and the ground. As a means of observing what was being done to his feet, it was both convenient and safe, for his arm shielded his eyes from Devlin's view. The disadvantage of the position was that his closeness to the ground robbed him of the ability to judge distance accurately. If Devlin put the gun to the ground, it would be infernally difficult to grab it in one movement. Cribb had something extra in mind.

The rope was now bound tightly six or seven times around his ankles. Devlin paused, ready for the crucial tying of the knot, his broad hands holding two loose ends and a gun, assessing the difficulty of manipulating all three. He passed the gun from the right hand to the left, held it thoughtfully for a second, and then put it on the ground beside him.

Cribb allowed him time to begin the process of tying the knot. Then he moved. In a sequence of actions so rapid as to seem simultaneous, he reached behind his head and fastened his hands on a carriage wheel for leverage, wrenched his bound legs from Devlin's grasp, drew his knees up to his chest and thrust his feet back at Devlin with all the force he could muster. It bowled the man off balance, and Cribb had dived for the gun and got it safely in his hand before Devlin lifted his head from the ground.

'Keep your distance, Mr Devlin,' he warned. 'It's a queer thing: since that knock on the back of my head, my fingers have started to twitch. Nasty affliction to have if you're holding a Smith and Wesson.'

Devlin lay as he had fallen, like one of the petrified inhabitants of Pompeii, while Cribb considered his next move. Things seemed to happen with embarrassing speed in the Secret Service. Masterly as his counter-plot was, and brilliant in execution, it had ended with possession of the gun. Now that he had a moment for reflection, he could divine certain difficulties in winning the confidence of the dynamite party with a loaded revolver in his hand. Still, he would not have made much of an impression either, tied up in the coach-house in shirt sleeves and socks. There was at least the opportunity now of making himself presentable. So, one-handed, he retrieved his braces, draped them over his shoulders and fastened them at front and back, a not inconsiderable feat. The waistcoat and jacket followed without fuss, and the hat, lodged firmly in place, and given a slight tilt as an afterthought. By George, he was ready to meet the dynamiters now! Or believed he was, until a slight coolness under the soles of his feet reminded him that he was still standing in his socks. Fortunately, the boots were of the button-fastening type, and quite quickly fixed. That done, he ordered Devlin to his feet. 'You were going to introduce me to somebody,' he told him. 'Isn't it time we went inside? There is really no need to hold your hands above your head like that. I didn't ask you to do that, did I? Just walk naturally ahead of me and don't try anything irregular on the way. I should greatly prefer it if you were still alive to make the introductions.'

With a nod more indicative of co-operation than comprehension, Devlin pushed open a door in the whitewashed wall on his left and led the way up some stairs and through a carpeted passage, Cribb keeping within two paces of him. A second door opened on to the entrance-hall of what was undoubtedly a house of considerable size. They crossed a tiled floor to an oak door, Cribb thoughtfully removing his hat meanwhile. Devlin tapped deferentially and pushed open the door.

Cribb followed him into a spacious, sunlit room, unexpectedly light after the panelling of the hall. In front of the mantelpiece, observing their entrance in a large gilt-framed chimney mirror, stood a young woman with copper-coloured hair formed into a tight bun on the top of her head. The moss-green silk of her tea-gown, a dress cut with such severity of line that the bustle seemed a subversive presence, betrayed not the slightest rustle of movement as she spoke. 'You have brought us a visitor, Patrick Devlin?'

Devlin cleared his throat. When his voice came, it was thick with the unease of his situation: 'I have, miss. His name is Sargent.'

'Why is he standing behind you?'

'Because of what he is holding in his right hand, miss.'

She shifted her gaze slightly, still looking into the mirror. 'A silk hat? What does that have to do with it?'

'There is something inside the silk hat, miss,' said Devlin, daring as much as anyone in his position could.

There had not been a hint of brogue in her voice before, but now she turned her face from the mirror and spoke in a broad Irish accent, wickedly mimicking Devlin. 'Indeed, and what might that be? Is it a little rabbit, at all?' She crossed the room for a better view of Cribb. 'Sure, I wouldn't have taken Mr Sargent for a magician.'

'Lord no, miss,' Cribb agreed, returning a grin. 'As you see, there's nothing in here but my hand. Mr Devlin is under a misapprehension. He thinks I am carrying a dangerous little article that belongs to him, but I left the object in question in the coach-house. I saw a convenient bucket of water and dropped it inside as we passed. You'll pardon me, I hope, miss, but I didn't catch your name just now.'

'It wasn't mentioned. I am Rossanna McGee.'

And a little over twenty years of age, he added in his mental notebook, with green eyes, dimpled cheeks and as white and even a set of teeth as you would wish to see.

By now, Devlin had turned round and was directing an avalanche of explanation on Miss McGee, who seemed more interested for the moment in taking a long look at Sergeant Cribb. '. . . And when he comes out of Malone's hotel,' Devlin said slowing his speech for emphasis, 'the first thing he sets his eyes on is our carriage, and he comes up to us at a trot and asks to be taken to Great Scotland Yard. D'you see now why I think your father should take a look at him?'

'What was that?' she said absently. 'Oh, Father. I shall go to him now and ask if he proposes to meet Mr Sargent. See that our visitor is comfortable, Patrick. *Try* not to behave like a jailor. He would hardly have marched you in here if he were thinking of running away.'

She left the room, and to encourage Devlin's confidence Cribb seated himself in a leather armchair. 'Handsome young woman, Miss McGee,' he ventured. 'Obviously Irish, but she doesn't show it in her speech. Not in the normal run of conversation,' he added.

'Rossanna had all her schooling in England,' said Devlin, emphasizing her Christian name as if he was wanting to make some point to Cribb.

'Ah, yes,' said Cribb. 'Elocution. Do you know, Mr Devlin, I sometimes wonder at the amount of time our better schools for young ladies devote to inculcating the Queen's English. But if she's lost her Irish accent, I dare say she's retained a proper interest in the cause.'

Possibly it was a too obvious attempt to draw Devlin. 'The cause?' he repeated vacantly.

'The deliverance of Ireland.' Heavens, he would need to be more subtle with Rossanna's father! 'Doesn't every young woman these days espouse a cause – married women's prop-erty, socialism and so forth? Seems sensible for an Irish woman to devote herself to Home Rule, if you see my point.'

If Devlin did, he was unwilling to enter into a conversation about it.

Cribb made one more attempt to elicit information. 'What kind of man is Mr McGee?'

'You'll see, soon enough.'

In seven minutes, in fact, by the skeleton clock under the dome on the mantelpiece. And when McGee did make his entrance, it was unlike anything Cribb could have prepared himself for. The leader of the infernal machinists, the father of the radiant Rossanna, was strapped into an invalid-chair, his head lolling helplessly forward as his daughter wheeled him into the room. 'Perhaps you were not aware, Mr Sargent,' she said, 'that my father, Daniel McGee, was the victim of an explosives accident eleven months ago. He lost the use of his legs and much of his face was blown away. That is why he wears this' She pulled the bowed head gently against the chair-back. It was covered by a black silk hood through which a pair of grey eyes regarded Cribb, the only certain indication of life. 'His jawbone was shattered, and the surgeons fixed his mouth in a permanently open position that an unprepared person would find grotesque and offensive. Because he can make only indistinct sounds you might think him an imbecile, but he is not. God in His mercy preserved my father's intellect. He will speak to you in the language of the dumb, by touching his hands on mine. There are some questions he wishes to put to you.'

Cribb had never experienced an inquisition like it. Inarticulate sounds issued from the hood as Rossanna's hands made contact with her father's and engaged in an elaborate procedure of clasping, tapping and stroking. 'My father wishes to be told the reason for your extraordinary interest in Mr Malone,' she presently said.

The two hours or so since his abduction had enabled Cribb to prepare for this. He had decided to keep his story as close to the truth as he could, in the interests of self-preservation. 'I was interested for my own reasons in making contact with the dynamite conspiracy. I had heard of an Irish-American called Malone who was seen in Rotherhithe

81

asking questions about the London stations shortly before the explosion in the cloakroom at Victoria last February. Malone is a common enough name among the Irish, I know, but when I chanced to notice it in a newspaper account of the Gaelic American Athletic Club's visit to England, I took more than a passing interest. It occurred to me, Mr McGee, what a brilliant strategem it would be to bring a group of dynamiters to these shores in the guise of sportsmen – perhaps even finding a first-class athlete who was interested in promoting the interests of his country in a practical way. So I decided to get to know Mr Malone better. I managed to insinuate myself into the party of Officials at Lillie Bridge, and I endeavoured to engage him in conversation during the hammer-throwing contest. When I found that he was not the sociable sort, I initiated a friendship with Mr Devlin here, thinking to learn what I could about Mr Malone at second hand. I was fortunate in being able to assist Mr Devlin in a small way to secure victory at Lillie Bridge—'

'I won the bloody contest outright,' Devlin interpolated.

'Unquestionably, but it required someone with my recently acquired knowledge of the rules to point it out. You were grateful at the time, which was fortunate for me, because you went on to tell me over a drink where Mr Malone's hotel was situated.'

'That was incautious, Patrick,' commented Rossanna.

'Faith, I was setting a bloody trap!'

'Quite right,' said Cribb. 'A possibility I had altogether failed to allow for. After I visited the Alcazar Hotel and found the management most uncommunicative on the subject of Mr Malone, I came out and was ensnared, as Mr Devlin has indicated.'

Rossanna put her face close to the mask and indulged in more finger-talk with McGee. 'My father wishes to know what you want with the dynamiters – if you are successful in finding them.'

Cribb permitted himself a slight smile at the addition, a touch of feminine caution, he was sure. McGee had a thoughtful interpreter. 'I want to join 'em, miss.'

An agitated session with the hands. 'My father asks why, when you are patently not an Irishman.'

'The answer is that I am a professional adventurer. I have a taste for danger, and I know a rare amount about the construction of infernal machines. I believe I could be useful to the dynamiters. And I don't mind admitting that I would expect to be well-paid for my services.'

Another consultation. 'Mr Sargent, my father thinks what you have said is presumptuous.'

'I'm damned sure the dynamite party can afford to pay me, miss.'

She tossed her head impatiently. 'He was not referring to that. He thinks it presumptuous of you to imagine that you can be of any use to the organization.'

Cribb raised his eyebrows. Inwardly his pulses were pounding. If he were not convincing now, they would undoubtedly kill him. 'I didn't come into this blindly, miss. I took a close look at what the dynamiters have done, and I know where they want some expert advice. Oh, I don't underestimate their ability, miss, or their pluck. And the machines are well enough made. It's the *positioning* of 'em that goes wrong. Take this latest group of bombings as an example. Four machines, of which only one does any notable damage, whatever the newspapers say. And one that doesn't detonate at all. I thought the reason for giving up clock-timing was to take the uncertainty out of detonations.' He raised a finger, warming to his theme. 'But setting that disappointment aside, it's a poor way to treat two well-constructed machines to put 'em in places where the best they do is frighten a few domestics and give the glaziers some work. Now a man with my knowledge of the metropolis – not to say dynamite – would have done a little better for the cause last night, I can tell you. Bang, bang, bang round the back of Downing Street, and Gladstone wouldn't be able to get to the House quick enough to introduce a Home Rule Bill!'

'You're not an anarchist, are you, Mr Sargent?'

'Not unless the money's right, miss. My affiliations are strictly on a mercenary footing. No, I tell you in all seriousness that what the dynamiters lack is the finishing touch. It's no good coming over from America – without offence to anyone here present – and leaving bombs at random all round St James's Square. My observations tell me there are three things lacking in the dynamite campaign: local knowledge, steady hands and the knack of putting bombs where they do the most damage. I'm the man to remedy those deficiencies – at a fee, of course. I was going to suggest a level pony – twenty-five pounds – for each successful detonation. Would you say that's a reasonable offer?' He addressed his question to the grey eyes behind the mask.

Rossanna put her head close to her father's and held his hands. More unearthly sounds proceeded from McGee. One thing was certain: no normal palate could produce such distortions of the human voice. Cribb waited, not knowing whether he was hearing an invitation to the dynamite party or a sentence of death.

Devlin approached the invalid-chair and murmured something – no petition for mercy, Cribb was sure. Rossanna drew away from her father. 'Mr Sargent, there remains a question to be answered. What was your purpose in telling the driver of our carriage that you wished to be conveyed to Great Scotland Yard?'

She put the question in a disarmingly mild manner, but Devlin's predatory stare from behind McGee left no doubt of the importance of the answer.

Cribb gave a deliberately naive reply. 'I thought it was a cab, miss.'

'One takes that for granted, Mr Sargent.' Her voice took on a more insistent tone. 'Why Great Scotland Yard?'

He grinned, as if he had some joke to share with her. 'Ah, I see your point entirely, miss. A pertinent inquiry, in the circumstances. The fact of the matter is that I'm a reader of *The Times*. Have you seen today's edition? There's a stirring account of the damage perpetrated in the capital last night. As one not uninterested in the fortunes of the dynamite campaign, I studied every word of it. What caught my eye in particular was a paragraph about the bomb discovered at the foot of Nelson's Column. Did you know that it was conveyed to Great Scotland Yard and left in the open for reasons of safety? They won't have it inside for fear of blowing up what's left of the Detective Department. So there it stands, miss, for anyone to see, and it's asking too much of a man as interested as I am in explosives to stay away. That was why the Yard was going to be my next port of call.'

Rossanna turned to Devlin. 'It appears to answer the point, Patrick. Mr Sargent would naturally be interested in seeing an infernal machine for himself.' Receiving no response, she addressed her father. 'What do you say, Papa? Is Mr Sargent to be relied upon?'

It was heartening to have Rossanna's support intimated, even if Devlin maintained a sceptical silence. The verdict that mattered, though, was being uttered from the invalid-chair. Understanding nothing of the inane sounds McGee was producing, Cribb studied the slits in the mask for some flicker of assent, and saw none. The only conceivable indication of what was going on was the movement of McGee's head, and when Cribb saw which way it was moving he preferred to regard it as a doubtful portent. Possibly, he told himself, the agitated conversation with the hands was rocking the chair.

It stopped. Rossanna faced Cribb. 'Mr Sargent, my father wishes me to inform you that he is interested in your claims, but not entirely satisfied of their veracity. However, he is prepared to give you an opportunity tonight of convincing him. You are invited to participate in a small expedition. It provides you with a chance to demonstrate the qualities of a professional adventurer. I take it that the prospect is attractive to you?'

'Shall I be paid for my services, miss?' Cribb asked, in a strictly professional manner.

She smiled for the first time. 'You will get what is due to you, Mr Sargent.'

Cribb decided he preferred Rossanna without the smile.

7

The sound of a church bell travelled across the water of Gravesend Reach. One o'clock. The last of a mass of cloud passed inland, uncovering the moon. The slate roofs and spires of Gravesend were picked out sharply in the swiftly-moving luminosity, as if the gauze was being drawn away in some transformation effect at Drury Lane. Certainly the night had a theatrical feel about it for Sergeant Cribb, leaning on the taffrail of a small steam launch chugging past the monstrous shapes of the merchant fleet, moored in readiness for the last few miles upriver on the morning tide. Whatever he had expected from the dynamite conspirators, it had not included a substantial supper, followed by a midnight outing on the Thames. After his ordeal in front of McGee, everyone – even Devlin – had made a point of being disconcertingly civil to him. As he had sipped claret and eaten cold chicken, he had been reminded of the cosseting of condemned men on their last night on earth. From there his thoughts had fastened morbidly on the late Constable Bottle being drawn from the Thames with grappling irons, an image that had been disturbingly revived after supper, when Rossanna had led the party out to a boat-house.

'Sargent!' a voice called from the direction of the cabin. 'Come below. Miss McGee wishes to speak to you.'

He answered the summons, careful as he descended the steps that no one *was* concealed on either side, waiting to crack him over the skull again with a blunt instrument. The twinges from the last battering were particularly acute in movements up and down stairs.

Rossanna was seated at a small table lit by an oil lamp. Facing her, more sinister than ever in this light, was Malone, who had joined the party after supper. Devlin stood at the wheel with his back to them. McGee had been left in the house, in the care of the functionary Cribb had taken for a cab-driver, but whose duties he now knew to include serving at table and ministering to the needs of the invalid.

'Please sit down, Mr Sargent,' said Rossanna, and added firmly, 'Here will do,' when Cribb was faced with the choice of sharing a bench with herself or Malone.

It was quite impossible to position himself on the narrow strip of bench without physical proximity of the sort one usually encountered in crowded third-class railway compartments – and then with nameless strangers. To accommodate her bustle, she was seated obliquely, and Cribb was obliged to adopt a similar position to avoid embarrassing contact with her knees under the table. In consequence, his legs were so restricted that he was sure his right thigh would touch her left if he leaned even slightly forward.

'Observe the map, Mr Sargent,' Rossanna ordered, as if divining his thoughts and indicating that she, at any rate, was too taken up with the night's business to be troubled by them. It was a chart of the river from Purfleet to the Estuary, and it was spread out across the table. 'We have just passed the Ovens buoy, marking Coalhouse Point, and this is the stretch of the river known as the Lower Hope. The place we are bound for is here.' She touched the map.

'Canvey Island?' said Cribb.

'Not quite, Mr Sargent. Look more closely.'

He was practically sure he felt the warmth of contact on his leg *before* he moved. 'A creek,' he said. 'Hole Haven. I can't say I've heard of it before.'

'Then you should read *The Times* more thoroughly. Hole Haven has more than once been referred to in the Parliamentary Report. Eight hulks are moored there. It is a desolate spot, accessible only by water when the tide is flowing, or across marshland from Canvey Island. Probably not more than a few islanders knew of the existence of the hulks until two of them were found unguarded three years ago. The owners were fined a total of over a thousand pounds for negligence.'

'Seems unaccountably excessive,' said Cribb.

'So one would have thought until 1882, when one of them, the *George and Valentine*, sank in Hole Haven. It was then revealed that it contained two thousand cases of dynamite, the property of Nobel's Explosives Company. Each of those hulks is a magazine, containing over fifty tons of dynamite.'

'Jesus!' said Malone, pulling excitedly at his whiskers.

'But where's the sense in it?' asked Cribb. 'Nobel's manufactory is in Scotland. What is the stuff doing in the Thames Estuary?'

'Waiting to be loaded on to outward bound vessels,' said Rossanna. 'They stop there regularly to collect consignments. It would be most unsafe, you understand, to have explosives stored in warehouses in the Port of London. Instead, they use the hulks in Hole Haven. Two of them belong to a German firm, the rest to the mayor of Gravesend, who receives the dynamite from Scotland and sees to the discharging, reloading and storage. An eminently sensible arrangement, and inexpensive, too. Each magazine, I understand, is guarded overnight by a single caretaker.'

'Holy Mother of God!' said Malone.

Rossanna was giving her attention to Cribb. 'So the purpose of the evening is to collect a modest consignment of dynamite from Hole Haven. It will be so much more convenient than making importations from America. In approximately three-quarters of an hour, Patrick will draw alongside the *Moravia*, the hulk least easily observed by coastguards, because it is partially obscured by two of the other vessels. You, Mr Sargent, and Mr Malone here will then board the *Moravia*, disincline the caretaker from interfering, and make a careful examination of the cargo. We shall not be able to take much away with us on this small craft, so we shall need to ensure that what we have is of the most powerful grade. You will unload six half-hundred-weight cases on to our deck and we shall gently cruise away with enough dynamite to bring down every bridge along the river if we feel inclined.'

'Now there's a grand conception!' said Devlin.

'Beautiful!' agreed Malone, half-closing his eyes to appreciate it fully.

'An illustration, merely,' said Rossanna. 'My father is planning something infinitely more dramatic and effective – provided that we obtain the means tonight.' She turned to Cribb again. 'We want no hitch in this little enterprise. You will follow Mr Malone's orders implicitly. In the circumstances, I have prevailed upon him not to carry a firearm, but he has no need of one when he can incapacitate a man just as quickly and more painfully with his bare hands.'

'There'll be no cause for that, miss,' Cribb promised her.

When he went on deck again, the winking buoy was well astern and the Estuary had broadened to more than a mile across. Devlin was steering close to the Essex shore, a desolate tract of marshland unbroken by any sign of habitation.

Rossanna's conference, disturbing as it was to anyone responsible for law and order, had rather fortified Cribb. His immediate future, at least, was less in doubt. The expedition was not planned with the sole intention of sending him the way of Bottle. Or so it seemed. If he were mistaken, it was the most diabolical charade-game he had ever taken part in. No, all the signs were that if he behaved convincingly as Malone's assistant that night, he would win the confidence of the dynamiters. Put it down to forethought, intuition or uncommon luck, he had offered McGee what the conspiracy lacked at this stage in its campaign: the professional touch. He might shortly be expected to demonstrate it. Lord, he was thankful for those weeks at Woolwich!

He was conscious of a movement at his elbow: Rossanna, holding something in her arms. 'Tall hats and morning suits look most distinguished, Mr Sargent, but they really will not do for climbing up the sides of dynamite-ships. Put on these things.'

He removed his hat and found it taken away in exchange for a bundle of clothes.

'Please do not delay,' said Rossanna. 'We are passing Shell Haven on the port side. Our destination is less than a mile away. Give me your jacket. I shall take it to the cabin.'

She was right; it was ridiculous to think of clambering aboard a guarded ship in morning-dress. The others were in jerseys and dark trousers. He unbuttoned the jacket and took it off, checking the pockets first – but all they contained apart from coins was a crumpled rosette. Rossanna took the hat and coat below.

She had left him with a woollen fisherman's cap – for which he was grateful, preferring not to go bareheaded out of doors, even in these circumstances – a black muffler and a short jacket in the reefer style. They effectively covered the telltale white and grey of his shirt-front and waistcoat. True, the reefer overlapped his shoulders and bulged somewhat in the area of his hips, but it was clearly made for a larger man. Now was not the time to fret over sartorial imperfections.

There remained something on the deck where she had deposited the clothes: a coil of rope, and under it, thoughtfully, a pair of black kid gloves. He slung the rope over his shoulder and was beginning to feel increasingly felonious, when his nostrils caught the whiff of something close at hand that quite restored the detective in him. Stale pipe-tobacco. It was coming from the clothes and he was absolutely sure that the brand was Marcovitch. He had smelt it a hundred times before. He ran his hands down the reefing-jacket, feeling its size and texture. Everything his pounding brain could suggest to check – buttons, pocket-flaps, lapels and vents – tended to confirm that it was Thackeray's. He searched the pockets, but they had been emptied systematically – or so it appeared, until his hand located a small ticket pocket on the left side. Inside was a railway ticket. He made sure he was not being over-looked and moved closer to the cabin to get sufficient light to examine his find. It was a platform ticket issued by the London, Brighton and South Coast Railway at London

Bridge station. The date on the reverse was 18 May 1884 – the Sunday he had found Thackeray beside the *Gladstone*. He knew, because he had a similar ticket in the pocket of his check waistcoat at home; when they had left the platform, there had been no collector on the gate. Numbed by a possible implication of his discovery, he replaced the ticket and stared unseeing at the dykes along the Essex shore.

'That's Canvey away to the right. This is Hole Haven,' Rossanna presently informed him. 'It looks a fine stretch of water, doesn't it? Half a mile, would you say? Moonshine, Mr Sargent. If we turned the helm now we should run aground. The only navigable part is a narrow channel running close to Canvey, and that is where Patrick is making for.'

When the launch did begin to leave the fairway, the hulks were already in view, moored close together in the shadow of a tall dyke that buttressed Canvey Island from the tide. A line of illuminated buoys served as a warning to other shipping, and seemed to have impressed the dozen or so craft seeing the night out in the channel, for they were anchored at respectful distances.

'We'll lower the funnel now,' Devlin called from the wheel. 'She's got a good head on her. We'll go in close, my darlings.'

The launch coursed steadily towards the dynamite flotilla, its own lights now extinguished and its crew alert for any sign of a coastguard vessel. Malone joined Cribb at the stern without exchanging a word. Now that they stood together for the first time, there was six clear inches difference in their heights. Cribb decided it was time to indicate his dependability. 'That grapnel you have in your hand, Mr Malone. Is it for securing a line to the *Moravia?*'

The big man gave the curt nod such an obvious inquiry deserved.

'In that case,' Cribb went on, 'perhaps you would allow me to be the first to go aboard. As the lighter man in weight, I should impose less strain upon the line, and when I get to the top I can ascertain that it is quite secure for you.'

Malone was sufficiently touched by this to turn his head and take a closer look at his assistant.

'I can shin up a rope as well as the next man and a little better than some,' Cribb added. 'I shan't keep you waiting long.'

'Very well,' agreed Malone, after considering it.

Devlin had already steered the launch between the buoys, and it was gliding noiselessly towards two hugely-looming hulks, the barnacle encrustments on their surfaces glistening in the moonlight. Cribb glanced towards the cabin. Somewhere in there was Rossanna, wrapped in a black shawl, scrutinizing every detail of the night's doings for her father. A hazardous duty that, for one of the fair sex, but from his observations he would wager that she was equal to any crisis the night would produce.

They passed under the bows of one vessel to the more sheltered side. The *Moravia* was ahead of them, secured by anchors at bow and stern, and lit by four lanterns. It was fortunate, Cribb decided, that Malone had got some practice, at least, at throwing the hammer. He did not like to speculate on the possible consequence of the grapnel striking one of the lanterns.

Devlin swung the wheel and they came alongside the hulk. Malone had moved forward and neatly fastened the painter to the aft anchor-chain of the *Moravia*. The launch came gently to rest against the vessel's towering side. Cribb waited for his companion to throw up the grapnel, hoping he had the wit to realize that on this occasion the object was accuracy, not distance. Happily it lodged neatly in position at the first attempt.

It was Cribb's turn, the chance to prove his usefulness. He took a high grip on the rope like a bell-ringer, tested the strength of the grapnel's hold and swung his legs clear of the deck, to clamp the rope between his ankles at the highest convenient point. In rope-climbing, the foothold is everything, as he demonstrated impressively, using the leverage of the thighs to gain height. It was an exercise he had not performed for a number of years, but one well-suited to his long, spare frame, as he had first discovered in his training for the military. Being ordered to demonstrate rope-ascents to the entire platoon at Canterbury barracks had more than compensated at the time for his ineptitude at foot-drill.

He reached the top in seconds, took a grip on the *Moravia*'s bulwark and clambered aboard. Momentarily, he crouched to recover his breath and relax his stomach-muscles in the way of a seasoned trouper who retires to the wings between displays of agility. He had not taken his second breath when he saw the feet.

They were wearing canvas shoes and coming fast in his direction along the deck. There was no time to take in the rest of the figure, but Cribb was in no doubt that it would be armed with some offensive instrument and he did not propose to present his still-sore head for further attention. Remaining in the crouched position, he tucked his right forearm between shins and deck and rolled rapidly over in the path of the advancing feet. It was like projecting a barrel down a ramp. The impact bowled the feet from under the figure and it crashed over Cribb's back. He threw himself upon it to crush any retaliatory move, but he need not have bothered. The body was inert.

Cribb examined the man – the ship's caretaker, he assumed – and found with relief that he was breathing, but unconscious. Probably his head had made connection with the bulwark on the way down; a fortunate circumstance, because it went against the grain to commit violent assault upon a man who was simply trying to do his duty, albeit with a particularly ugly-looking belaying-pin. Cribb did not pause to moralize longer, but set about tying the hands and feet of the caretaker with the rope he had brought. As he finished the job, Malone's head appeared above the bulwark. 'What happened?' he asked Cribb in a stage whisper, then saw the caretaker on the deck and exclaimed, 'Moses! You're a sharp mover. We were supposed to tackle the bugger together.' He heaved himself on to the deck, leaned over to signal to the launch that all was well, picked up the belaying-pin and wrenched a hasp and padlock from the hatch with prodigious ease. Cribb was thankful he had dealt with the caretaker himself. He might so easily have become a party to murder.

Malone swung back the hatch and descended a ladder into the hold.

'Can you see all right?' Cribb inquired into the darkness.

'Don't touch the lanterns!' Malone cautioned in a whisper that was probably heard on Canvey Island. 'It's here, by Jesus. Crates of the stuff. You'd better come down.'

Cribb obeyed, and when his eyes adjusted sufficiently for him to find a way between rows of boxes stacked three high, he joined Malone, who was already pushing one towards him.

'Half-hundredweight crates, just as she said,' he told Cribb. 'Take the other end, will you? We can't be too careful with this stuff.'

They shuffled along the aisle to the ladder and by degrees got the crate on deck. In the moonlight, the mark of the Nobel Explosives Company was clearly visible on the lid under *a Danger-Explosives* warning.

'There's some letering here,' said Malone. '*N.G. 75.* Is it a code, at all, d'you reckon?'

'Seventy-five per cent nitro-glycerine,' explained Cribb.

'Holy Father! All this lot and only one caretaker! It's a public scandal!'

'Report it to your Member of Parliament,' Cribb suggested dryly. 'Hadn't we better collect the other crates meanwhile?'

They returned to their removals and within a short time had the full consignment of six ready for loading on to the launch. Malone appeared quite breathless at the end, a development which could hardly be put down to want of strength. Cribb could think of only one explanation: the man's nerves were troubling him. Strange, for a dynamiter. Perhaps the knowledge of what a little of the stuff could do made him uncomfortable in the presence of so much. His hands were definitely trembling as he passed his length of rope around the first crate to secure it for the descent.

Cribb peered over the side. Devlin, below, returned his wave. For stability, Malone wound the loose end of his rope once around the ship's rail and pulled it taut. 'You'd better hold the line,' he told Cribb. 'I'll lift the crate carefully over. Be ready to take the strain when I tell you, for God's sake.' He picked up the crate as if it were a sleeping baby and gently lowered it over the side. 'Now!'

It was less difficult to control than Cribb expected, possibly because Malone was draped over the rail steadying the rope. Less than half a minute later came the easing of tension that meant it had arrived on the launch. Devlin released the rope and they repeated the operation with the second crate.

The third was the one that transformed everything. It was halfway down its twenty-foot descent when something – a turbulence in the water, or a moment's loss of concentration by the handlers – started it swinging. There was a sickening thud as it hit the side of the hulk, followed by another, less powerful. 'God in Heaven!' Malone suddenly shrieked in alarm. 'It's slipping the rope!' Half a hundredweight of dynamite was going to crash on to the deck of the launch and he was manifestly unwilling to wait for the result. He had scrambled over the railing and hit the water before Cribb, still holding his line, felt the loss of resistance indicating that the crate was no longer at the other end of it. A stifled scream from Rossanna was overtaken by a crash and the sound of splitting timber. Nothing worse.

Somewhere nearby, voices were shouting questions into the night. Malone's cry of panic had raised the guardians of the other hulks. Cribb crossed to where the grapnel still supported the line he had used to board the *Moravia*, and let himself down with a little less elegance than in his military heyday. The shattered crate had spilled cartridges of dynamite over the deck of the launch. Devlin had been knocked aside and was picking himself up.

'Are you fit?' Cribb asked.

'I think so.'

'Get to the wheel then and get under way. I'll see to this.'

'Is it safe to handle?' asked Rossanna, coming from the cabin.

'Yes,' said Cribb, 'but I must move the pieces away from the engine-room. One spark . . .'

'I'll help you.'

The shouting on the sister ships continued. Someone was using a lantern to flash signals to Canvey Island.

Devlin raised the funnel and the launch throbbed into life. A shout close at hand distracted Cribb. Malone, his mop of hair flattened seal-like to his head, was trying to clamber aboard.

'He can hold on,' said Rossanna, but Cribb thought otherwise and moved to give assistance. The waterlogged hammer-thrower was four times as heavy as the crates and quite a different undertaking, but by brute strength and simple mechanics Cribb engineered him into a position where he could topple over on to the deck.

The launch weaved between two hulks and made for the open river, listing precariously as Devlin swung the wheel. Rossanna helped Cribb cover the crates with a tarpaulin. A voice was appealing to them through a megaphone to declare their identity, even though it was fast becoming obvious that they were not much interested in replying. The caretakers' isolation in their different vessels had brought an encouraging element of confusion to the scene. The coastguards, when they came from Canvey, would get half-a-dozen conflicting accounts of the raid.

Cribb joined the others in the cabin. Malone had shed most of his sodden clothes and was getting dry by shovelling coke into the boiler. 'Once we clear the Haven we'll have a flood tide with us,' called Devlin. 'No one's going to overtake us then.'

'They may not overtake us, Patrick,' said Rossanna, 'but if someone has the wit to use the telegraph, there could be a coastguard launch coming to meet us from Gravesend. If we get home tonight, it will be more than we deserve. And I do not relish telling my father that his plans were frustrated by a shameful exhibition of panic.'

'We got some dynamite,' said Devlin in mitigation.

'Less than half the amount we came for.'

'The crate was slipping,' said Malone defensively. 'It might have blown us all sky-high.'

'And who was supposed to have secured it?' Rossanna demanded in a fury. 'Are you admitting to incompetence as well as funk? Did Mr Sargent here scream like a school-girl and jump into the water? No, he kept his head.'

'Rossanna, don't get in a wax,' said Devlin. 'We'll think of something to tell your father.'

Cribb wondered what. It would be disturbingly easy for Devlin to shield Malone by blaming the newcomer for the imperfections in the expedition. He hoped he could rely on Rossanna.

When the launch headed towards the Lower Hope and began to make swifter progress, the tension aboard eased perceptibly. Malone borrowed Devlin's coat and went forward to keep watch for any sign of a coastguard boat. Rossanna drew her shawl moodily about her and went aft.

'Ah, that's a fine woman,' Devlin said to Cribb in the cordial vein of their conversation at Lillie Bridge, as if any unpleasantness between them was forgotten, 'but she bears the devil of a lot of responsibility. It doesn't do to cross her when she's implementing her father's plans. Since the accident, she and McGee have been very close. Understandably. She was always sympathetic to the cause, but it didn't go to anything more adventurous than joining the Ladies' Land League until McGee practically blew his head off trying to make a clock-timed machine. It looked as though the whole campaign had floundered before it had got under way. He's the brains, you understand. Malone and I are very minor in the organization. Then word came from New York that we were to take our orders from Rossanna, she being able to interpret her father's statements to us.'

'But it isn't always practical for McGee to be present,' Cribb observed, 'and who gives the orders then?' He knew the answer, but he was interested in Devlin's reaction to the question.

'She's every bit as forceful as her father,' said Devlin. 'I don't know whether it's the Irish blood or the red hair, or both, but she gets her way, Mr Sargent, she gets her way.'

'Pardon me for smiling,' said Cribb. 'It's a queer sight to an outsider – two sturdy fellows like yourself and Malone taking orders from a slip of a girl like that. I should have thought one of you might have had his hand around her waist by now. Isn't she susceptible to manly charm?'

'I told you,' said Devlin. 'She's devoted to her father. It might be difficult for you to apprehend, but there it is. Besides, Malone and I are here to do a job. There'll be women enough when we get home.'

'I'm sure,' said Cribb. 'Believe me, I wasn't questioning your loyalty to the cause, or your manhood. I was merely curious to know why Miss McGee has just gone forward to join Malone.'

101

He got his answer within seconds. It came in the form of a pistol-shot that echoed across the waters of the Lower Hope.

'Lord! Has she gone mad?' exclaimed Cribb. He left the cabin and ran to where she stood with smoke still rising from the revolver in her hand. Malone lay dead at her feet.

'Get him over the side, Mr Sargent,' she told Cribb matter-of-factly. 'Ireland has no need of cowards'

Cribb had never been so close to murder. Constable Bottle had died like this. Perhaps Thackeray. So incensed was he that he acted instinctively, regardless of how an agent of the crown conducted himself. He wrenched the gun from her grasp, flung it down and took her by the shoulders. 'That was a lunatic thing to do, Miss McGee, a monstrous, callous act. I'll not demean myself by throwing insults at a woman, but, by God, I know what you are now, and what you deserve. Get below, before I thrash you.'

8

'Nobody ever spoke to me like that except my father,' said Rossanna as she heaped devilled kidneys on to Cribb's plate. It was 6 a.m., and he was seated at a bare wooden table in the kitchen of the dynamiters' house. Much against his expectation, they had passed through Gravesend Reach and got back without further incident. Devlin, with the strain of the night's doings written on his face, had gone straight to bed. Rossanna had confounded Cribb by meekly offering to cook him breakfast before they retired.

The first shock of Malone's sudden dispatch had passed. It had been the fact of murder more than any sentiment about the hammer-thrower's going that had prompted Cribb to react so impulsively. Malone had not been one of the most endearing representatives of his race, and it had been more fatiguing than distressing consigning him to the Thames. There had been time after that, as the launch steamed homeward, to consider how a secret agent might recover from such a lapse.

'You were absolutely right, of course,' Rossanna continued. 'I should never have fired the shot. I didn't give a thought for the dynamite on board. Ridiculous! I might have killed us all.'

'You understood my reason for speaking to you so strongly, then?' said Cribb, with resource.

'Graphically, Mr Sargent. I am at a loss to understand how you exercised such restraint. I deserved nothing less than the chastisement you were ready to inflict on me.'

An exceptional development. Far from the hostile reaction he had expected, she seemed to have warmed towards him.

'Aren't you going to have some kidneys, Miss McGee?'

'I wasn't intending to – but if I might be so bold as to take one from your plate, it would give an opportunity of talking to you a little longer.'

'Please help yourself.'

She gave a tentative smile, and forked a kidney from his plate. Then she sat opposite him, turning the fork speculatively in front of her. 'You were magnificent tonight, Mr Sargent. I shall be reporting favourably to my father.'

'I'm glad to hear it,' said Cribb.

'Do you know what most impressed me? It was when you remained completely calm when the crate fell. Nine men out of ten in your position would have followed Malone into the river. Panic is extremely contagious.'

'You're right,' said Cribb. 'We were in more danger from ourselves at that moment than we were from the crate. Dynamite can't be exploded by ordinary concussion, and that's been proved. There were tests carried out some years ago in Wales – Glynrhonwy Quarry, Llanberis. Half-hundredweight crates were dropped repeatedly 130 feet on to broken shingle and none of them exploded. Then they dropped a box filled with two hundredweight of slate rubbish on to a crate of dynamite. Same result. It requires a sharp, smart blow on a thin coating of the stuff between two pieces of iron to set it off. The nitro-glycerine which it contains has no means of escape from the effect of the blow.' His tutors at Woolwich would have been proud. Rossanna looked slightly bemused.

'So that was why you kept a cool head?'

'In a nutshell, miss, I've got a strong instinct for survival, but I don't like getting wet unnecessarily.'

'Do you know why I shot Malone?'

'Because he panicked?'

'Yes – and because he was of no further use to us. There was nothing he could do that *you* could not do equally well. Perhaps better.'

She eyed him with such intensity over the fork that he decided it was time to divert the conversation. 'I'm not much good at hammer-throwing.'

'Nor was he. Paddy Devlin is the hammer-thrower. Malone needed an alibi, being Irish-American. You don't. When we've all had some rest, I'll tell Papa of the part you played tonight. I don't think he'll entertain doubts about you much longer.' She began fingering the fastening on the back of her hair. 'It's time I was in bed, Mr Sargent. I'm suddenly quite tired. But not displeased. I hope you are not.' On cue, her hair cascaded over her shoulders, gleaming red and gold in the early morning sun.

'On the contrary,' said Cribb spiritedly.

'Might I ask one favour of you before I go – to share a secret with me? I told Patrick that Malone turned the gun on himself tonight – from shame, you see – and I shall tell my father the same. I don't deserve it, but *please* may I count on you?'

Cribb gave a solemn nod.

*   *   *

105

Considering his situation, he slept well, disturbed only by occasional unfamiliar sounds from the drive below his window. The latest of these, the rasp of carriage wheels, drew him from bed. From between the curtains, he watched the manservant struggling to unload a portmanteau from the roof of the four-wheeler. One portmanteau was much like another, but Cribb was privately satisfied it was the one he had seen and left alone in Malone's room in the Alacazar Hotel. Someone had been remarkably quick to take account of the night's events.

He turned from the window. There was sufficient light without drawing the curtain to permit a more thorough examination of the room than he had made on being shown into it eight hours before. The shape was determined by one of the twin gables fronting the house; a man of his height had to keep to the middle or duck his head. But it was still furnished more lavishly than any police section-house he had slept in. Discipline in the Force was not to be undermined by brass bedsteads with feather mattresses, marble washstands and Turkish carpets. Cribb did not feel threatened by a few creature comforts. Not even a dressing-table.

It stood in the corner farthest from the door, white in colour, with sprays of forget-me-nots painted on it. The skirt of white muslin that should have been suspended from the edge of the table-top had been removed, perhaps out of regard for the feelings of the new occupant, and the legs underneath looked disturbingly exposed. There was a square mirror above, with adjacent flanking mirrors. Cribb approached to a position where he could see himself in triplicate. The profile on the left, he decided, had a shade more of the dynamiter in it than the full face or the opposite profile, particularly when he pushed his lower lip forward. It was still difficult to think of himself as Malone's replacement. He decided to look again when he had changed out of his borrowed nightshirt. Some clothes had thoughtfully been left out for him.

There was a cold luncheon waiting when he got downstairs and found the dining room. The factotum served it without a word, and withdrew, leaving him to help himself to cheese and fruit. He enjoyed an unhurried meal, and ventured through the adjoining conservatory into the garden. Noticeably overgrown lawns sloped from the house to an orchard, beyond which gleamed the Thames. Hearing a slight cough, he strolled in that direction.

'Ah, Mr Sargent,' said Rossanna. 'I was wondering whether we should see you. You feel refreshed, I hope?'

'Famously, thank you, miss.'

'Please call me Rossanna.' She spoke from a hammock slung low between two apple-trees. Dappled sunshine played over her gently oscillating form, dressed for the afternoon in ivory-coloured cotton lawn, trimmed with lace. Her father sat near by in his invalid-chair, a wide-brimmed straw hat angled so that it obscured the top of his mask, without interfering with his vision. 'And have you taken lunch?'

'I have, thank you.'

She smiled in that way that, rightly or wrongly, seemed charged with ulterior meanings. 'Then you cannot possibly have anything to do but talk to me. It is time we got to know you better, don't you agree? If you go back to the conservatory, you will find a cane chair. Bring it out in the sunshine, Mr Sargent, and place it just there under the tree, where we both can see you.'

He was not deceived by the casual charm of the

invitation, nor the setting. Every move he had made since coming downstairs had been artfully contrived to get him into the garden in a compliant frame of mind. She had staged it all: the solitary meal, the open door into the garden, the cough to catch his attention, McGee silently present, herself indolently posed in the hammock, waiting for him. It was different only in detail from being dragged struggling into a room and roped to a chair. The interrogation in the next two hours was no less searching or persistent. Her thoroughness in extracting every detail of his story would have provided an object-lesson for any aspirant to detective work. The Clan-na-Gael was not proposing to admit a novice to its ranks without first sifting his personal history over and over for the possibility of deception.

Cribb, for his part, was not unprepared. He had decided to apply a principle that had served him well in his selection interview for the C.I.D. six years before. He would give so much prominence to the things his questioner wanted to hear that anything adverse would be crowded out. Of course, it was difficult crowding out an entire career in the Force, as distinct from a few minor insubordinations, but the principle was there. After a substantially accurate account of his childhood, he waxed eloquent about his army days, making three years sound like the greater part of his life. From there, he moved deftly on to his career as a mercenary, careful not to include any detail that could betray him. His knowledge of dynamite, he explained, was gained in Paris, in service with the anarchist movement. The names of Kropotkin and Malatesta rolled from his tongue as naturally as the words of the official caution to prisoners – thanks to some profitable reading at Woolwich.

In 1882, he said, he had severed his links with the Black International, after the arrests of Cyvogt and Kropotkin, and returned to London.

If Cribb thought his recital was over, Rossanna did not. She continued to press him for more information, verifying dates, names and places. The questions followed no logical sequence, but tested his story at every conceivable point. He was forced to take chances, and more than once faltered and desperately hoped she and her father would put it down to lapses of memory.

'Thank you, Mr Sargent,' she finally said. 'You must think me the most inquisitive woman alive.'

'Good Lord, no, miss,' Cribb gallantly replied. 'Anyone in your father's position is entitled to make reasonable inquiries about a person in his employment, and I'm sure you were putting the questions on his behalf. I'm a professional man. I don't object to such procedures.'

She smiled. 'Then you will understand that I must now confer with my father. Would you be so kind as to help me to the ground?'

He took her hands and drew her forward. She swung her legs clear of the hammock and stood upright, so that he felt the touch of her dress against his legs. He made to take a discreet step back, but she continued to hold his hands, momentarily detaining him. 'You are more than kind,' she said, and then went to McGee.

When the dumb-language was done, Cribb saw with satisfaction that her expression was still friendly. 'Father has asked me to take him indoors now,' she told him, 'but there are things I must say to you, important things. If you will wait here for me, we can take a turn around the garden in a few minutes.'

Leaning there against the apple-tree while Rossanna wheeled the invalid-chair towards the house, Cribb tried to account for the peculiar effect he seemed to have on her. A man the wrong side of forty needed to guard against miscalculations where young women were concerned, but he was strongly of the opinion that she was making overtures to him. It was not the sort of thing one was accustomed to, working for the Yard. He supposed adventurers encountered it more often, by the nature of their work. That rope-ascent the previous night had been a stirring demonstration of agility, he was bound to admit. Yet he would have thought the brutal dressing down he gave the girl after she shot Malone would have put a stop to any sentimental stirrings. Not at all: it seemed to have stimulated them. The breakfast she had cooked him, the unpinning of her hair, the invitation to use her Christian name had not indicated much hostility or resentment. Nor had the business beside the hammock.

The odd thing was that Devlin had given the impression that the girl was exclusively devoted to her father. The presence of two strapping young athletes in the house had not moved her in the least. One way of accounting for it was that she was play-acting, coldly and deliberately putting the recruit through some kind of test. The only other explanation Cribb could supply was that she was one of those unusual members of her sex uninterested in young men, preferring to submit to the authority of older, more masterful partners. To such women, a reprimand was an affirmation of affection. He pulled a leaf off the tree and thoughtfully dissected it.

She came across the lawn again in a muslin shawl she had not been wearing before. 'Being so near the river, we get droves of gnats and flies invading the garden late in the afternoon,' she explained. 'It invites disaster to walk about with one's arms exposed.' She linked her left hand lightly and naturally under his right forearm and they set off slowly in the direction of the river-bank. 'Do you know what impressed Father most about your story? You made no claim at all to be a patriot of Ireland. That would have been the most obvious way to curry favour with us.'

'I told you,' said Cribb in his most masterful manner, 'I'm a mercenary. A professional adventurer. I don't care a tinker's damn for Ireland unless the money's right.'

'It will be. Tell me, Mr Sargent, have you ever heard of the Skirmishing Fund?'

Cribb shook his head. 'Can't say I have.'

'Then I must educate you. It is a sum of money which has been raised in America by public subscription, to finance the skirmishing of England until Ireland gains her freedom. It was started some years ago in the columns of a New York newspaper, the *Irish World*, by Diarmuid O'Donovan – the Rossa, as he is known.'

'The Fenian,' said Cribb.

'The same. We don't talk much of Fenians now, Mr Sargent. They were totally discredited when the Rising failed in 1867. Imagine the incompetence of an organization which postpones its revolution and fails to get the information to County Kerry! The men of Kerry had captured a coastguard station and a police barracks before they discovered their mistake and had to be sent home. And when the Rising did take place three weeks later it was in a blinding snowstorm and never looked like succeeding. You may still hear talk of the Fenians, but the organization is dead. There is only one revolutionary body of any importance, and that was founded in 1869, when most of the Fenians were in prison. Clan-na-Gael is its name.'

'Clan-na-Gael,' repeated Cribb ingenuously.

'It is pledged to deliver Ireland from the English oppressors,' said Rossanna, squeezing Cribb's arm at the thought. 'In 1877 it gained control of Rossa's Skirmishing Fund, which now amounts to not less than a hundred thousand dollars.'

'Good Lord,' said Cribb. 'That's a lot of subscriptions.'

'A lot of Irish-Americans have suffered at the hands of the English, Mr Sargent. What you would refer to as the Irish Famine, people like my father remember as the Great Starvation. Every concession since then, every clause in the Land Act, is written in the blood of Irish patriots. England has given us nothing we have not fought for tooth and nail – nothing that is, except rack-renting, evictions, Coercion and the Crimes Act.'

'You were telling me about the Clan-na-Gael,' Cribb reminded her firmly.

She regarded him intently. 'You're right. I keep forgetting that you have no affiliations. The Clan? It is a massive organization, Mr Sargent, with camps in every city of importance in America. It has rituals and proceedings which every member is bound to keep secret, under penalty of death. But if you wish to be one of its agents, you will have to join.'

'I'm not in any position to refuse.'

'Then we shall arrange it soon. There are ways in which you can be of important service to us. Four years ago O'Donovan Rossa broke with the Clan. It was not doing enough active work for his taste and there was even talk of a pact with Parnell and the parliamentarians – the New Departure, as it became – mere peddling with reforms. Rossa gathered together what was left of the old Fenian Brotherhood and organized raids on public buildings in Britain, mostly with gunpowder. The explosions at the Glasgow gasworks and the Local Government Board were the work of the Rossa agents. It was all handled with the usual Fenian ineptitude. Ten of them were captured and brought to trial in Edinburgh at the end of 1882. Five got penal servitude for life, the rest seven years. Another four of Rossa's men were arrested after one of them was found with the infernal machines upon him as he stepped from the Cork steamer on to the quay at Liverpool. They each got a life sentence last July. It was the finish of Rossa's campaign.'

'I'm not surprised,' said Cribb. 'Fourteen convictions is not the sort of record that encourages recruitment.'

'Rossa is a spent force,' Rossanna went on. 'There is too much of the Blarney about him. He served his purpose in raising the Skirmishing Fund, but he should have left the active campaigning to men like my father. Fortunately, the Clan is better organized. Our dynamite policy was authorized in November 1881, at our National Convention in Chicago, but it wasn't until the end of 1882 that the first agent of the Clan travelled to England to inaugurate the campaign. The organization was in the hands of the Revolutionary Directory and the agents were selected and trained in America. The selection had to be most carefully done, because we had information that forty of the Royal Irish Constabulary had been sent to the States on full pay with the object of insinuating their way into the Clan.'

'Diabolical!' said Cribb.

'It didn't happen, Mr Sargent. Soon enough, parties of trained men were crossing the Atlantic with the means to cause havoc in London. The first was led by Dr Tom Gallagher, with his brother Bernard and six others in support. Tom, being the swell he is, set up residence in the Charing Cross Hotel in the Strand, while the others frequented small hotels and retired lodgings in the south of London. Before long, as the world knows, they had established a nitro-glycerine manufactory in Birmingham and were conveying the stuff to London in india-rubber fishing boots contained in boxes. It was pure chance, a singular catastrophe, that caused a Birmingham detective to have his suspicions aroused and visit Whitehead, the chemist of the party. Tom and two others as well as Whitehead were convicted and gaoled for life, thanks to the testimony of the wretched Mr Norman.'

'They say there's no Irish conspiracy without its informer,' said Cribb, piously shaking his head.

'The Clan know how to deal with traitors,' said Rossanna. 'Shall we take this path along the riverside? There are some water-irises further on.'

'By all means,' said Cribb, wondering at the nature of a woman whose thoughts shifted so easily from dynamite to flowers. It was a narrow path leading past the boat-house where the launch was kept, and a larger building beyond. From this came the sound of hammering. Four men in labouring clothes were outside, lifting a large sheet of metal from a stack.

'What's going on?' Cribb asked.

'They're working with Patrick. It's a job for my father that required additional help, so Patrick and Tom recruited some loyal Irishmen at a public house in Rotherhithe. We pay them better rates than they would get working on the docks and boatyards, and Patrick brings them down-river on the launch each morning. They don't come into the house at all. Now who was I speaking of? Ah, yes. Poor Tom Gallagher. He was carrying £1,400 of the Fund when he was arrested. The Clan doesn't believe in under-providing for its agents.'

'I'm glad to hear it.'

'The only other Clansmen to have been arrested are John Daly and Francis Egan, who are still awaiting trial at Warwick. John's plan was to toss a bomb on to the table of the House of Commons from the Strangers' Gallery while the House was in session. It sounds desperate, but he twice gained admission to the Gallery and would have had a well-made brass bomb with him the third time. He was carrying three when he was stopped at Chester railway station in April. But there are still two other groups besides our own at liberty.'

'When did your father arrive in England?'

Her expression softened. 'Last year – in May. He was to establish himself here well in advance of Devlin and Malone's arrival. The house was placed at the disposal of the Clan by a patriot who owns another place in Surrey. He was good enough to leave one of his staff behind as well, a man who can be depended upon in every sense. It was his summons which brought me here from America after Father's accident.'

'That was in June?'

'What an excellent memory you have – yes. He was testing a small bomb here in the grounds when it detonated prematurely, with terrible results. He was the Clan's principal machinist. Despite his injuries, he is carrying on the work.'

'With your help.'

'That is so.'

They stopped to watch a hay-boat pass along the Reach, its brown lateen sail catching enough wind to give it the advantage over a toiling lighter laden with bricks. Cribb decided the time was ripe to extend the conversation. 'Two of the groups in custody, you say. This is dangerous work. Would any of the convicted men inform on us?'

'They don't know where we are. It is the policy of the Clan that the groups work independently. We all have our instructions from America, and we are here to carry them out without reference to anyone else. In the last year that I have been working for the Clan, I have not met any of the men who have been taken. Everything I have told you about them you could have read for yourself in the newspapers.'

This was true. 'So that when a bombing takes place it is just as surprising to you as it is to the public at large?'

'Exactly – unless we have arranged it ourselves.'

'Was it yours in Scotland Yard the other night?'

She smiled. 'I'm sorry to disappoint you. It was not. Nor were the others that night. We are here for something altogether more ambitious.'

'Isn't Scotland Yard enough?'

'There are more important targets than that, Mr Sargent.'

He wished Inspector Jowett took the same view. 'The police are sure to intensify their inquiries. Have they any knowledge of our existence here, do you think?'

'I think not. Not now.'

'That sounds significant.'

She shrugged her shoulders. 'One night when Malone was at the public house in Rotherhithe he got into

116

conversation with a man he suspected was a police agent. This was at the time of the London station explosions – which this group was not responsible for, I might add – and the man was interminably talking about locomotives and timetables. Malone suspected he was trying to feed us false information, but when we checked some of it we could not fault him. Then one night we discovered that he was being watched by the police – a Special Branch man, as we discovered. Malone lured this one into a trap and shot him.'

'Ah.' How else could Cribb react, except privately to note that Malone's own death had been no more than he deserved for killing Constable Bottle? He asked, as casually as he was able: 'And the other man?'

'We brought him here. He saw the shooting of the Special Branch man, you understand.'

'Of course. Did you . . .?'

'Not yet. We think our locomotive enthusiast has some useful information for us. He *must* be a policeman. He possesses all the characteristics, from the thick skull to the flat feet. He was probably wanting to sell information to Malone. They aren't paid much at Scotland Yard, you know. The Special Branch man must have suspected what was going on, and consequently followed them into the trap. If the Special Branch were interested, then he *has* got something to tell us, and he is in no position now to demand a fee. We'll get it from him soon, and then Father has something else in mind for him. He will be incorporated into the plan.'

Whatever that was, it did not matter for the present. Thackeray was alive – thick-skulled, flat-footed and breathing!

'You have this man here? I haven't seen him.'

'You won't, Mr Sargent. It is better for us all if he is kept locked away until we are ready to use him.'

117

'Quite so. Are you sure you can handle him, though? Without Malone's assistance, I mean.'

'Perfectly sure. He is no trouble.'

From her manner, she wanted to drop the subject. It would have been incautious to press her further on the matter of Thackeray, tantalizing as it was.

'Pardon me for asking,' Cribb said, as they turned in the direction of the house. 'Is it usual for the Clan to employ members of the fair sex?'

She laughed. 'Not so unusual as you might think, Mr Sargent. We are not the insipid creatures some of you men take us for. The Ladies' Land League was a far more militant organization than the men's, until Mr Parnell got cold feet and insisted upon its dissolution. Besides, modern fashions give us a distinct advantage over men in conveying dynamite secretly to England. How do you think Atlas Powder travels – in men's trouser pockets?'

'I'd never considered it,' said Cribb candidly.

'Then take my advice and have nothing to do with strange women on ocean-going steam-ships, unless you are prepared for a devastating experience.'

Cribb laughed. 'Not the kind you have in mind, Rossanna.'

At the mention of her name, she tightened her grip on his arm. 'If you were wondering about me, I promise you I have nothing under my skirts to alarm you, Mr Sargent, if you are the man I take you for. I believe you described yourself as an adventurer.'

Heavens! She was at it again, more flagrantly than before. And looking damnably fetching at the same time. He took a long, uplifting breath. 'That's correct. But I did say a *professional* adventurer, and it occurs to me that I might still

118

be on probation, so far as the Clan is concerned. I'm here in my capacity as a dynamiter, nothing else. In other circumstances, miss . . .' he added gallantly.

They walked the rest of the way across the lawn in silence, Cribb trying to convince himself that it was just another phase of the inquisition. He would have felt eminently pleased at the way he had come through it, if only the inquisitor hadn't looked so damnably disappointed.

9

Cribb quietly locked his bedroom door from the inside, withdrew the key and pocketed it. He crossed to the window, pushed it up and looked down at the conservatory roof, ten feet below. After the Alcazar Hotel, this promised to be child's play. He picked up a length of rope he had earlier scavenged from the coach-house, and firmly secured one end of it to the door-handle. The other he dropped over the window-ledge, leaning after it to see how far down it extended. Far enough for a controlled descent to the frame of the conservatory roof. He tested the strength of the rope, seated himself on the sill, swung his legs over and turned inwards, shifting the weight of his body on to his stomach. Gripping the rope ahead of him, he began to let himself down.

It was after two in the morning, an hour and a half since he and Devlin had retired, and they had been the last to go up. Rossanna had gone first, soon after eleven, leaving the others at a poker game. 'Our river trip last night has quite upset my routine,' she had announced. 'If I don't retire at once, I shall fall asleep in my chair. Too ridiculous for words! I shall probably wake up in the small hours wanting breakfast when everyone else is deep in slumber. Are you an early riser, Mr Sargent? You look as though you might be. Patrick *ought* to be, as a sportsman, but he never stirs before nine when he is staying here, do you, Patrick? And Father sometimes sleeps until noon. Well, you need not tell me, because I shall hear for myself. My room is on the first-floor landing and I know every loose floorboard in the corridor above. When I hear you, I shall know that I am no longer the only one awake in the house.' Cribb had not been sure whether she said this to discourage initiatives by night, or the reverse. At any rate, he had decided already that he would have to find a way downstairs that did not bring him into contact with the floorboards, and that was why he was once again performing on a rope.

He lowered himself to the level of the room below his and paused there, trying to see in. It was a first-floor bedroom, unoccupied. He could have forced an entrance through the window if he had wanted, but all it contained, he suspected, was Malone's luggage. Certainly it had not been inhabited in the last twenty-four hours. Tonight he was looking for Thackeray, not infernal machines.

His feet touched the conservatory roof, lighting safely on one of the wooden crossbeams. The structure was sturdy, well able to support his weight. Leaving the rope dangling, he crossed the roof to a section where it overhung the main entrance, inset between the two gabled wings at the front of the house. On his level, there were the windows of the main first-floor landing. He went confidently to one he had unfastened earlier from the inside, eased it open and climbed into the house again.

During the period after dinner he had occupied himself profitably by making a mental sketch of the lay-out of the bedrooms. The second floor, where his own was, had one other, the manservant's, built in to the gable opposite.

The floor below housed Devlin, McGee and Rossanna, as well as the empty room below his. It was quite impossible, he had decided, for Thackeray to be imprisoned on the first or second floors, for every other room could be accounted for as a bathroom, linen-room or water closet.

There was something else that encouraged him to concentrate on the ground floor. While Rossanna had been cooking those devilled kidneys, he had noticed four trays set out on the dresser, obviously in anticipation of breakfast. Three were matching in design, finely lacquered and laden with expensive porcelain and silver. The other was made of plain, unvarnished wood and there was a tin porridge-bowl on it and a mug, of the sort provided in common lodging-houses. At the time, Cribb had taken them for the manservant's. Later, he reflected that someone eating in the kitchen had no need of a tray; he would eat from the kitchen table. The probability was that it was for Thackeray. If so, it was not unreasonable to suppose that the place where he was confined was directly accessible from the kitchen. A tray of that description, without even a cloth on it, would have been glaringly conspicuous in any other part of the house.

He pulled the window gently closed and glided towards the stairs. His movements were confident. He had tested the boards on this floor very thoroughly earlier in the day. They were firm under his weight, not straining to betray him like those upstairs. Rossanna, even if she were awake, could not possibly know that he was passing within a yard of her door. Just the same, he drew a long breath when he was safely clear. The danger of McGee's door opening, or Devlin's, troubled him less than hers. He moved smoothly past and down the stairs. Without pausing, he crossed the tiled hallway to the dining room and so made his way into the kitchen.

It was darker there than it had been upstairs. The moonlight was all on the other side of the house. He hesitated at the threshold, remembering the myriad of objects he might dislodge from shelves and hooks and send crashing to the slate floor. By degrees his eyes adjusted to the conditions. It was a large room, dominated on one side of the table by the range, and the other the dresser, fairly bristling with crockery. The four trays were set out ready for the morning, as before. Other objects, an ironing-board, a tin bath and a meat jack threatened to raise the house if he should accidentally knock them down. It was fortunate that he had not marched blindly in, because there were two fly-papers suspended near the dresser at the level of his head. He would probably have reacted to the unexpected contact by flinging out his arms in self-protection.

Two other doors led off from the kitchen: one, the tradesmen's entrance, looked on to the kitchen garden; the other promised to be the scullery. He pushed the door behind him shut and froze in his tracks. Something soft had touched his back, moving rapidly across the width of his shoulders. He wheeled round, and was confronted with a large canvas string bag, swinging gently from a nail on the back of the door. He grunted and moved decisively across the kitchen to the scullery.

A cat came to meet him as he opened the door, and smoothed its fur against his legs. He swung his eyes swiftly around the room. Dresser, sink, door, copper, mangle, door. The second door was the one that interested him. It probably led to a store for fuel or provisions, but it was bolted at top and bottom. He approached it and slipped the bolts. It opened easily. The cat ran inside. Cribb followed.

It was pitch-black. He whispered, 'Thackeray?'

Not a sound.

'Thackeray!'

A muffled groan from somewhere to his left.

'Where are you, man?'

Thackeray's voice, just coherent, said, 'Can't you perishers let a man have a wink of sleep?'

'It's me. Cribb.'

'Blimey!' A fumbling and scratching was followed by the striking of a lucifer, which immediately went out. 'Blooming cat!' A second attempt was successful. The lighting of a candle revealed the shaggy countenance of the constable who had once helped to arrest Charlie Peace. He was lying on a bed improvised from sacks stuffed with straw. Bundles of firewood were stacked on all sides of him. 'Sarge, how did you find me?'

'Never mind that,' said Cribb. 'Keep that candle away from the cat. This place is a blasted tinder-box. Now, Thackeray, are you all in one piece?'

'Just about, Sarge, but I've had enough of this. I've been incarcerated here for two days with only a supply of candles and a Bradshaw's *Guide* to keep me from going barmy. They bring me food twice a day and I can use the privy in the garden after nightfall – under escort, of course – but it ain't my notion of a bank holiday weekend. Strewth, I'm glad you've come along to get me out of it.'

'I haven't,' said Cribb. 'I just dropped in, so to speak.'

Thackeray's jaw dropped. 'Do you mean that I'm not getting out, Sarge? Are you going to leave me here?'

'I've got no choice. Freeing you would give the game

away. They think I'm on their side, you see. I won't forget you're here though, depend upon it.'

This solemn assurance seemed to carry little weight with Thackeray. You could have driven a cab through the gap between his moustache and beard.

'So we must make the most of the time we have,' continued Cribb. 'I want a brisk account of how they got you here and what they've told you. Pull yourself together, man, and make your report, or there'll be something on your defaulter sheet at the end of the week.'

The cold sponge treatment worked best with Thackeray. 'I'm sorry, Sarge. I was lying here thinking of a warm feather bed when you came in.'

'And I've left one to come and talk to you. Get on with it.'

'Well, I was right about Malone,' said Thackeray. 'He proved to be a regular scoundrel. Not many days after our meeting at *The Feathers* he came in again. I managed to engage him in conversation and led him to believe that I was sympathetic to the idea of Irish independence. In fact I went so far as to say that a few bomb explosions round London might blast some sense into Mr Gladstone and encourage him to introduce a Home Rule Bill. I wanted Malone to feel that he could impart confidences to me, you see.'

'Did he?'

'Not in as many words, Sarge, but he seemed to look upon me as a useful companion, and I was able to tell him quite a lot about the sights of London. He took an uncommon interest in such monuments as Nelson's Column and the Albert Memorial. The thing that impressed him most of all was a mention I made of the Tower Subway under the Thames. Coming from America as he had, he hadn't heard of its existence, so I promised to show it to him last Friday.'

'The night you were captured?'

'Yes. We had a drink or two and I was confident that he was ready to talk about the dynamite conspiracy. We started on our walk and presently he told me that he thought we was being followed. To tell you the truth, I didn't take much notice. I didn't reckon any of the Bermondsey roughs would waylay a hulking great bloke like that, even if he was a blooming Irish Yankee. It was getting late when we passed into the tunnel from the Pickle Herring Street end, and we was the only ones inside except this geezer behind us. If he was following us, he couldn't make a secret of it there, because it's only seven feet wide, as you know. Suddenly Malone says, "Let's stop and see how close the bastard comes." Before I know what's happening, he's produced a big American revolver and shot the poor perisher through the head.'

'What did you do?'

'I said, "You've killed him," and he laughed and said it was only a bloody copper and that he'd fix me too if I didn't hump the body back to Bermondsey. So I did, at gunpoint, and all the way up the blinking spiral staircase, so as to dump it in the river. Then bless me if he didn't march me down Shad Thames to a steam-launch, order me aboard, tie me hand and foot and leave me in the care of another Yankee, name of Devlin. I was brought here and given the candles and the Bradshaw and that's almost all I can tell you, Sarge.'

'You haven't been interrogated yet?'

Thackeray went a shade paler. 'What's that, Sarge?'

'Questions.'

'By George, yes, I've had Devlin in here three times and a very violent man he is, I can tell you. It ain't Queensberry's rules in this house, by any manner of means. If you was looking for a split lip or a black eye you won't find them, but I could show you marks in places no prizefighter ever had to worry over. Some of them was inflicted with the sharp end of that young woman's parasol too, while Devlin had me pinioned on the sacks here. She ain't so delicate-minded as she looks, Sarge, believe you me.'

'Are you badly hurt?'

'I don't think there's any permanent damage, but I wouldn't like much more of it. I haven't told them anything. Perhaps I should. They seem to know most of it already. They keep wanting me to confirm that I'm in the Force. How could they have discovered that? You don't think I should tell them, do you?'

'No – not if you can help it. When were they last here?'

'I think it was yesterday morning. Fortunately, they seem to have plenty of other things to do as well. There's no end of work going on in that big shed at the bottom of the garden. I can hear it each time I get taken outside, and that's after dark. Is it infernal machines, do you think?'

'Could be. What's that?' He had heard a movement somewhere overhead. It was repeated. Footsteps, he was certain. 'I've got to be off. Now listen, Thackeray. You and I have stumbled upon a plot that promises to be more barbarous than anything the dynamiters have done so far. For some reason, they've taken it into their heads to make use of you. When the time comes, co-operate. Take no account of anything untoward you might see me do. I shan't intervene until the moment I judge right, and I want no half-baked heroics from you. Do you understand?'

'Yes, Sergeant.'

'Goodbye for now, then. And Thackeray, try to keep your wits about you.' He had gone through the door and almost closed it when Thackeray's urgent shout arrested him.

'Sergeant!'

'What now?'

'You forgot the blooming moggy.'

'Perishing animal!' He reached in, caught the cat by the scruff of the neck and launched it across the scullery. It touched down with a yowl and took cover behind the mangle. He closed the door of Thackeray's prison and fastened the bolts. The object of the mission was achieved. There only remained the matter of getting back to his room.

If somebody upstairs was on the move, did it follow that they would be making for the kitchen? Cribb decided he could only wait and see. By remaining where he was, he *might* escape discovery altogether. At the worst, he would hear the other's approach and give nothing away of his own presence until the last possible moment. It gave him the chance to prepare a reception.

He walked to the kitchen door and listened. All was quiet so far. He dipped his hand into the bag of string and selected a fifteen foot length, free of knots. To one end of this he tied a kettle. He then opened one of the windows on his left and gently lowered the kettle to the concrete path outside, making no sound. He pulled the window almost closed, leaving enough room for the string to have free play across the sill. He unbolted the kitchen door and opened it wide. The cat streaked across the room to freedom. Cribb took up a position behind the door through which his discoverer would come. He had the string in his left hand and a rolling-pin in his right.

A minute passed before anything happened. Then came the tell-tale squeak of a floorboard in the room next door. Cribb tensed, watching the door-handle. It turned, with excruciating slowness. Lord, the reception would have to work well!

The door began to open, with obvious caution at first, then, as Cribb had hoped, swinging rapidly inwards. The first thing the intruder would see was the open door to the garden, facing him. Cribb jerked at his string. The kettle outside clattered on the path, suggesting someone had just dashed out there and kicked something, in his hurry to be gone. Caution abandoned, the would-be pursuer surged across the threshold. Cribb swung the rolling-pin towards its mark. In the split second before it connected, he made the satisfying discovery that it was destined for the head of Patrick Devlin. He levelled the score.

There is no reliable way of knowing how soon a man crowned with a rolling-pin will regain consciousness. Cribb did not intend to stay to find out. Pausing only to kick Devlin's Smith and Wesson out of sight under the dresser, he left the kitchen and hurried through the dining room and across the hall to the stairs. He mounted them two at a time. On the way, he took the key of his bedroom door out of his pocket. This was not the occasion to be suspended on the end of a rope; he would risk the floorboards instead and get back to his room by the conventional route.

It was a simple enough intention, but he was unable to carry it out. Halfway along the first-floor corridor, on his way to the next flight of stairs, he distinctly heard movements overhead, borne down by the eloquent boards. Someone else had been disturbed – the manservant. What deplorable luck!

As if this were not enough to give a man apoplexy, there came sounds from downstairs. Devlin had recovered and was coming at speed through the dining room.

There was no question now of taking to the rope from the conservatory roof. He did the only thing possible in the situation: opened the door nearest to him, stepped inside and closed it. It was Rossanna's bedroom.

He stood just inside the door, trying to estimate the effect of his sudden entry. What does a woman do when a man bursts into her bedroom in the middle of the night – scream blue murder or become paralyzed with fright? Nine women in ten, he guessed, perhaps ninety-nine in a hundred, would do one of those things, but he could not be sure about Rossanna. From what she had said earlier in the evening, she might have been lying awake listening for movements. In that case, it was possible she had heard what *he* had – the creaking boards upstairs – and put a different construction on the sound. Could she actually have been expecting him? Was she lying there in anticipation of a development she regarded as the logical consequence of having a mature professional adventurer in the house? If so, it was one thing they had *not* prepared him for at Woolwich Arsenal. But it did provide him with a means of sanctuary. If Devlin came knocking at the door, she was not going to reveal to him that she had a secret visitor – not if she was quickly reassured of the nature of the visit. It rested with Cribb to provide such reassurance. There was not much time for it.

Better not speak too loudly. He took two measured steps

in the direction of the bed. The room was so dark that every movement was a small adventure. Her scent, the fragrance of stephanotis, lay on the air, increasing his unease. A Scotland Yard career was no preparation for boudoir atmospheres. Still, he was determined not to forget that he represented law and order; without that, his present situation was unthinkable. He was doing this for the protection of the realm. After what Thackeray had described, he certainly had no inclination to be here for any other reason!

His hands touched something cold and hard: the foot of a brass bedstead. He gripped it strongly and spoke in a subdued, but resolute voice: 'Such a warm night, Rossanna. Couldn't sleep at all, so I've risen early. No notion of the time, I'm afraid, but I remembered that you said you'd be awake in the small hours. Thought I heard a movement down here, so I came to see if you were wanting company. Not that I want to impose myself. You'd quickly tell me if I wasn't welcome, wouldn't you?'

He paused for a response, but got none. She could not possibly still be asleep. He could only interpret silence as encouragement. He edged along the side of the bed for Queen and country. 'You needn't be afraid of me, you know,' he continued. 'I ain't the sort to force myself on one of the fair sex, not if it ain't by invitation. But I've knocked about the world a bit, young Rossanna. Paris . . . Berlin . . . I think I know how to treat the ladies as they like it. Here, let me hold your hand for a moment. Pretty little hand it is, too.' He put his right hand confidently on the bed. Finding nothing, he moved it towards the centre. Still nothing, and what was even more disturbing the bed was cold. He felt with both hands. Great Scotland Yard! He had addressed the most passionate speech of his career to an empty bed!

Where the devil was she, then? As if in answer, he heard her voice from the corridor outside. 'So it was you, Patrick! I was wondering what on earth was happening downstairs. I was really quite frightened. I went up to Mr Sargent's room for protection, but he is fast asleep with his door locked.'

'Are you sure?' said Devlin. 'Well, if it wasn't him, somebody must have broken in. I found the kitchen door open and I thought I heard them running off. There was more than one, I reckon.' His voice hesitated, plainly baulking at the full account of what had happened in the kitchen. 'What were they after, do you suppose?'

'I really wouldn't know. Is the prisoner secure?'

'Quite safe. I checked him.'

'Good. And the back door – is it locked now?'

'I think so. That is, I can't remember.'

'Really, Patrick! What's come over you? You must be sharper than that, you know. Go down and make sure, and we can all get some sleep. I shall be locking my door, like Mr Sargent.'

Suddenly, Cribb was profoundly reluctant to be discovered in the bedroom. The situation had altered totally. He wheeled round in desperation, and discerned the dark shape of a door beyond the bed. He opened it and passed through, just as the handle of the other door was being turned.

He found himself in the next bedroom, better lit because the curtains were made of some thinner material. The air seemed fresh after the scent-laden atmosphere next door. He tiptoed towards the door, so determined to get quickly out and upstairs that he gave only a passing glance to the figure in the bed.

A glance he was not to forget. It discovered McGee, for once without the black mask. The dynamiter's grey eyes stared piercingly from an agglomeration of scar-tissue and raw-red flesh, pitted and contorted beyond belief. Except for the eyes, the only approximation to a human feature was a cavity on the left side, held rigidly agape and twisted at the extremity into a hideous leer. It was a more dreadful testimony to the effects of dynamite than anything Cribb had witnessed on the bomb-ranges at Woolwich. Most chilling of all was the knowledge that McGee was awake and must have recognized him, seen him come from his daughter's bedroom, and been unable to utter a coherent word of protest. The recriminations would have to wait.

Without turning round, Cribb opened the door and emerged in the corridor. Heedless of the floorboards now, he mounted the stairs to the top floor, arrived at his room, unlocked it, slipped inside and locked it again. He went to the window and hauled in the rope, reflecting as he did so that he might as well have made a noose at the end and put it to personal use. After this night's doings, there was not much to choose between that and a bullet in the head next morning.

10

It took a long bout of hard thinking to get Cribb down-stairs for breakfast. Whichever way he reviewed the night's events, he came back to the penetrating scrutiny of the grey eyes in that mis-shapen face. They had fastened on him like the eyes of the Argus. It was only with a consummate effort of concentration that he managed to dispel the idea that everything he had done that night was known to McGee.

The facts, when he finally disentangled them, were not quite so depressing. Nothing was known to the dynamiters of his meeting with Thackeray. Devlin had merely checked that the prisoner was still in his cell; it was enough to know that he had not escaped. Rossanna seemed to have convinced herself that because Cribb's room had been locked, he must have been asleep inside, and not down-stairs. The disturbance in the kitchen had been put down to some amateurish attempt at house-breaking. For his own reasons, Devlin had mentioned nothing to Rossanna about the bruise he undoubtedly had on the back of his head. Left to them, the capers in the night were quite likely to be forgotten.

With McGee, it was different. There was no escaping the fact that he had seen Cribb pass through his room. What mattered was how he accounted for it. In his pessimistic turn of mind the previous night, Cribb could think of no other construction than the true one: that he had gone secretly downstairs, been disturbed by Devlin and managed to avoid him by hiding in Rossanna's room and escaping by way of her father's. Constable Bottle had been shot for less.

In the morning, though, a happier theory emerged. It started in a curious way. He was sitting on the end of his bed, reflecting on the seriousness of his position, when he was unexpectedly dazzled by the morning sun, beaming in through the open window. He moved out of its direct line, and was reminded of his interrogation in the orchard. At one point in the afternoon the sun had caught the side of his face, causing it to feel quite uncomfortably warm. He had resisted the impulse to move because Rossanna had been so particular about the placing of his chair. It had to be in a position where her father could observe him. And now, with the powerful insight of a man threatened with extinction, he realized why. McGee was deaf.

It should have been obvious before. Damage to the eardrums is a common enough consequence of bomb-blasts, and McGee's other injuries proved how close to the blast he had been. What was more, he used the deaf and dumb language, and significantly, so did Rossanna when she was addressing him. For the rest, he had to lip-read. That was why the placing of the chair had been so crucial: it had to be set so that he was given a clear view of Cribb's mouth.

If this were so, then McGee's interpretation of the previous night's doings was limited to what he *saw*; he must have been oblivious of the commotion downstairs and Rossanna's conversation with Devlin in the corridor. He

135

had simply seen the man he knew as a professional adventurer come out of his daughter's bedroom and walk quickly through to the corridor. If he had a quarrel to make, it was as an outraged father, rather than the guardian of the dynamiters' secrets. But with a daughter like Rossanna, what else did he expect from a professional adventurer?

So Cribb stood before his dressing-table mirror, confirmed that he had the look of a man of the world from at least one angle, and went confidently down to breakfast. Devlin and Rossanna were already giving their attention to generous cuts of grilled steak, topped with an egg. The servant hustled out to attend to Cribb.

'How mistaken I was!' said Rossanna. 'I took you for an early riser, Mr Sargent.' She was wearing a high-necked green silk blouse and black velvet skirt. Her immaculate hair emphasized that she, for one, could not be accused of having lingered overlong in bed.

'I'm sorry. You must have been waiting for me,' said Cribb.

'Not at all,' said Devlin. 'Nobody stands on ceremony here, as you'll find out. If Rossanna and I had got a decent night's sleep like you, we'd still be in bed ourselves.'

Cribb took the cup of tea Rossanna poured for him. 'Was there something that disturbed you, then?'

She smiled. 'A small alarm in the night, Mr Sargent. Patrick surprised somebody in the act of breaking in through the kitchen. We have decided that it must have been a less than competent burglar – someone from the village probably.'

'We shan't be calling in the law to investigate,' added Devlin with a grin.

'Did you see them?' asked Cribb casually.

'I was just too late for that. Next time, perhaps.'

'Gracious! I hope it won't happen again,' said Rossanna. 'I was thoroughly alarmed by it all. I felt so unprotected when I heard Patrick go downstairs that I wrapped my dressing-gown around me and went up to your room to see if you were awake. You must be a deep sleeper.'

'Like the dead, once I'm off,' said Cribb without hesitation. 'I'm sorry about that, though. You should have given me a shake. Ah, but I think my door was locked. A professional habit from my anarchist days. It was more to protect me from my fellow revolutionaries than from the authorities. Give an anarchist a chance and he'll preach the social revolution all night long. That's why they're all narrow-eyed and pale of face, did you know?'

She laughed. 'I wonder what you say about the Irish.'

'Nothing like that, I promise you,' said Cribb. 'You don't look deprived of sleep, Rossanna.'

She coloured slightly at the compliment and pulled at the curl that lay against her right cheek. 'I think my father must agree with you. After we were all disturbed, he detained me for at least three-quarters of an hour. Conversation with the hands is quite fatiguing at half past two in the morning, particularly with an agitated parent.'

So McGee had lectured her already, asked her to account for the man in her room!

'Did you manage to reassure him?'

She paused. 'Eventually. He really had no need to be agitated.'

'I appreciate that, miss. It was all cry and no wool, as the devil said when he sheared the pigs.'

She put her hand to her mouth and giggled briefly. 'Mr Sargent, you do say some droll things!'

At least she was showing no hostility. Far from regarding the night manoeuvres as evidence of treachery, she seemed encouraged by them. Whatever her father had said, it must have convinced her that the visitor to her room was there by choice. 'It's a very old expression, Rossanna. I was referring to the fact that the intruder, whoever he was, didn't get what he came for.'

This provoked another fit of giggling. Cribb, who had not intended to be facetious, looked Devlin's way and shrugged his shoulders. He was pleased to see that the Irishman appeared uncomprehending. If Rossanna had told *him* what her father had seen, he might have divined the truth.

'Enough of last night, gentlemen,' said Rossanna with a decisive change of tone. 'I have an announcement of unusual importance to make. You will know that when my father arrived in London last year, it was to set in motion a plan so brilliant in conception that the Revolutionary Directory of Clan-na-Gael agreed to make available enough of the Skirmishing Fund to cover all our expenses for an indefinite period. A party was selected from the most experienced agents in America, each chosen for the special contribution he could make to the project. The most ingenious arrangements were devised to introduce these men into Britain without arousing the suspicions of the Secret Service. For reasons of security, only one member of the party, my father, was entrusted with the full knowledge of the plan, and he was its architect. The rest of us have had to be content to wait until our contribution was required. And stage by stage it has taken shape before our eyes. Of course, there have been setbacks, as there are in the execution of any project so beset with dangers. My father's dreadful accident was the first, but we overcame it, and the rest – the loss of Tom Malone and the harassments from the Special Irish Branch of Scotland Yard – were of little consequence by comparison, particularly as you arrived at so timely a moment, Mr Sargent.'

Cribb accepted this small bouquet with a nod.

'Well, gentlemen,' Rossanna went on, 'let us be forthright with one another. We have all been waiting with impatience for the orders that will initiate us into the final mystery – the ultimate object of all our work. The preliminaries are over. We have collected enough dynamite to destroy any building in London. Your many months of labour in the workshops are complete, Patrick, and your team of assistants has been paid and dismissed. Father has told me that his hours of consultations of maps and charts have yielded the information he requires. Yesterday morning, gentlemen, two emissaries of the Revolutionary Directory arrived at Liverpool in the steamship *Alaska*. They are senior officers – not merely black-baggers. Their decision will give the final authority to the plan.'

'The darling gentlemen!' said Devlin with feeling.

'When shall we see them?' asked Cribb, with all the enthusiasm at his command.

'Tomorrow evening. They have convened a formal meeting of the Clan. It will give us the opportunity of admitting you to our ranks, Mr Sargent. That is essential if you are to join us in the climax of our work. I assume that you have no objection to taking a solemn oath to devote yourself to the cause of a free Ireland?'

'I'll swear to anything, miss, if I'm paid for it.'

'That isn't what our visitors will want to hear, Mr Sargent, but Patrick and I understand the conditions of our arrangement with you, and as my father is proposing you, there should be no difficulties. However, he is most desirous that you should make a good impression on them. Coming as they do, fresh from America, they will not have heard of Tom Malone's passing, rest his soul.'

'Amen,' murmured Devlin, nodding his assent like a man at a prayer-meeting.

'It will undoubtedly come as a shock to them. Their first inclination might be to cancel the project.'

'The buggers!' said Devlin.

'But we shall then tell them of the more than adequate substitute we have found.' She indicated Cribb with a wave of the hand. He returned a modest smile.

'And that is the juncture,' she continued, 'at which Father has decided you will do something that will leave no doubt in their minds as to your eligibility for the Clan.'

Cribb's smile faded. 'What's that?'

'You will provide a demonstration of your bomb-making skills. You are to use the time between now and tomorrow evening in constructing two infernal machines. We shall detonate one of them in full view of our guests in the most dramatic circumstances. It will reinforce all the fine things Father will have to say about your usefulness to the Clan. Isn't it a splendid plan?'

Cribb took a fortifying sip of tea.

Before he could respond, Rossanna went on, 'The second machine, which must be identical to the first, will be required later on. You shall have all the materials you need. Tell me, how much dynamite would you say is necessary to destroy a building of moderate size – say the size of Patrick's workshop in the garden?'

Devlin was on his feet. 'What the blazes—'

'Don't get so agitated, Patrick. I am merely providing Mr Sargent with an example. Well?' She raised her eyebrows and looked in Cribb's direction.

He tapped his nose knowledgeably. 'Hm. It's a brick building if I remember. Solidly constructed. Fifteen pounds of the stuff would certainly do it, though, and you might manage with less. It depends very much on where you place your charge.'

'We shall come to that in a few minutes. Finish your breakfast, Mr Sargent, and you may then escort me into the garden. There is something I must show you. This is just the morning to be outside, don't you agree?'

In five minutes, she was steering him determinedly into an area of the garden they had avoided in their previous walk, a wilder, more wooded part, where she had to lift her skirt to avoid entangling it in briars. Cribb picked up a stick, trimmed it and used it to beat away obstructions. When they had been going some hundred yards and the house behind them was out of sight, Rossanna gave a small cry of distress. 'My skirt! It is all caught up on a beastly bramble, Mr Sargent.'

He turned from his beating and went to her aid. It was difficult to account for the accident. He had been most conscientious in clearing every hazard from the footpath, even to the point of slashing the stems of those liable to spring back. For all his efforts, she was undeniably held captive at the side of the path. 'You should have kept to the centre, Rossanna,' he told her. 'Now keep still. It's not the skirt that's caught, it's the petticoat. My word, lace as delicate as this wasn't made for promenading in the woods, you know. If you'll just move your foot a fraction to the right, then – oh, my stars!'

How it happened, he was not clear, because he was too occupied stooping to disentangle the lace from the bramble without damage. He was briefly aware of a quivering movement from Rossanna. She wobbled, changed her footing, reached out with her arms and then lost balance altogether, gently subsiding into the fronds of young bracken behind her. It would have been passably discreet if one of her hands had not caught Cribb's shoulder and toppled him over in the same direction. His fall, too, was gentle. He found himself immersed in a sea of lace and white linen, his right hand in contact with a stockinged knee and the side of his face pressed against an area it did not take a C.I.D. training to identify as her bosom. In trying to extricate himself, he inadvertently brushed his left hand across a surface of smooth, warm flesh terminated by what could only be a garter.

'Then you *did* come to my room last night!' exclaimed Rossanna, without displaying much concern at her predicament. 'I was sure I heard you move across the floorboards on your way back to bed. No wonder Father was so restless!'

'I'm not sure what this has got to do with it,' said Cribb, lifting his head, but refraining from any further movement of the hands.

'I should have thought it was obvious,' said Rossanna, giggling. 'I hope your bomb-making is more restrained than your love-making, Mr Sargent, or we shall all be blown up when you get to work with the dynamite this afternoon. Much as I am flattered by such a display of passion, I must plead to be released on this occasion. There is so much to be done before the emissaries arrive tomorrow, and Father relies on me absolutely.' She lifted her head and pertly kissed the tip of his nose. 'Perhaps in a day or two, when

142

the work has been completed . . . Now, if you will kindly put down my skirt and help me to my feet, we might resume our walk.'

The whole thing had happened so precipitately and without any initiative on his part – whatever she suggested to the contrary – that he felt quite weak at the knees when he stood up. If, as he suspected, she had engineered it all, then she was a remarkable young woman, a conclusion he had reached soon after meeting her, without realizing *how* remarkable. But why should she have arranged such an accident? Was it to satisfy herself that he had really been on an amorous mission the night before? She had certainly reacted emphatically after the accidental arrival of his hand upon her thigh. Accidental? Fortuitous, more like. She had taken it as the signal of a resumption of passion. It was all she had wanted to know.

Satisfactory as the outcome was, he still felt that his reputation as an adventurer was a little tarnished by the incident. He reflected, as he obligingly removed a thistle from the back of Rossanna's skirt, that a professional would not have behaved in quite the same way. And he would have struck a short, sharp blow in that area to rekindle her respect for the adventuring profession if she had not been wearing a bustle.

As it was, they continued their journey along the path for another hundred yards or so, when they came to a small lake. On the far side was a tall red-brick tower in the gothic style, crenellated at the top. It was accessible from the bank on one side, but supported in the water by three arches.

'What's that?' asked Cribb.

'A folly, Mr Sargent.'

'Folly?'

'A useless building erected at the whim of a landed gentleman. Some call them gazebos. This one is your target for destruction.'

'Good Lord! The owner won't take kindly to that, will he?'

'The owner is an Irishman. He will be told that his folly was sacrificed to the cause. I am sure you must have destroyed scores of buildings more serviceable to mankind than this monstrosity.'

'Yes indeed,' said Cribb, remembering himself. 'But won't the noise attract unwanted attention from people hereabouts?'

'It is most unlikely. We are quite isolated here. If anyone heard a distant explosion they would assume it came from the cement workings at Stone. Blast the gazebo out of existence, Mr Sargent. Your reputation depends upon it.'

11

The rest of that day and the next was a period of intense activity in the house by the river. The impending arrival of the emissaries from the Revolutionary Directory had galvanized everyone. Formal meals were abandoned. Nourishment was snatched at irregular intervals. What consultations there were took place in corridors and on staircases, and were confined to essential business.

Cribb, not least, needed every minute he could get at his work. Three weeks at Woolwich had given him a useful grounding in explosives, enough to pass muster among the dynamiters, but no one at the Arsenal had envisaged him *making* infernal machines. He had to make them now, or confess he was an impostor. To complicate matters, Rossanna had insisted that the gazebo be destroyed from underneath, by a charge placed in a water-tight metal box at the base of one of the brick supports. He had tested the depth of the water there with a stone and line and found it to be over nine feet. The pressure of the water at that depth would assuredly curb the destructive power of the dynamite; how much, he could not begin to assess.

There was no shortage of bomb components. Devlin took him to an out-house beside the kitchen-garden and unlocked the door to a veritable arsenal. As well as the cases of dynamite from Hole Haven, there was at least a hundredweight of Atlas Powder stored there. 'I shall need some detonators,' said Cribb, trying not to seem staggered at the force represented in the store. 'You can't make bombs without detonators.'

'We keep them elsewhere,' said Devlin, giving him a long look. 'I'm not the authority on explosives here, but I'm told you don't store detonators with dynamite.'

'Oh, quite right,' Cribb airily conceded. 'Where are they, then?'

'In the house. We keep them in the room under yours.'

It was said in the matter-of-fact manner that could not possibly be taken for anything but literal truth. This was shortly borne out, when the two men entered the room in question. The first thing to take Cribb's eyes was the mantelpiece. Anyone unfamiliar with the manufacture of infernal machines might have wondered at the lengths to which some people go to bestir themselves in the morning, for at least a dozen alarm clocks were crowded on the shelf. Cribb crossed the room and picked one up. 'Benson of Ludgate Hill, eh? Nothing less than the best.'

'McGee's orders,' explained Devlin. 'He blames his accident on a faulty clock. The detonators are over here, in the tallboy.' With conspicuous care, he pulled open a drawer. Three rows of test tubes lay on a bed of cotton wool, each one held fast by a twist of wire. 'Malone did all this. I don't know what the stuff inside is.'

'It must be a fulminate of some kind,' said Cribb. 'Probably mercury. What's in the other drawers?'

Devlin opened one to see. 'It looks like a rope to me.'

Cribb turned a piece over in his hand. 'Slow-match. This

146

is what I'd use to make a bomb in the normal way. It burns a yard in eight hours, compared with the yard a minute of a conventional fuse. Unfortunately, you can't burn a slow-acting fuse in an airtight box, so I'm restricted to a clock-timed detonation. Do we have guns?'

Devlin opened the other drawer.

'Cartridge-firing pistols,' said Cribb, glancing inside. 'You can see why so many of the bombs deposited about London never go off. There's too many possibilities of faults in the mechanism. If there isn't something wrong with the alarm-clock or the connection with the trigger, there's still the possibility of the hammer not striking the cap truly, and missing fire. It goes against all my bomb-making principles to make a machine as liable to defects as that and then drop it into nine feet of water and expect it to detonate perfectly. It's too much to expect.'

'My heart bleeds for you,' said Devlin, with a grin that suggested otherwise. 'Those are the watertight boxes beside the wardrobe. I think you'd better start work at once. The Clan doesn't look kindly on failures.' With that, he left, presumably to check that his own work was in order.

Cribb, in sole occupation of the room, and with the key to the dynamite-store in his pocket, allowed himself a moment's reflection. He had secured a position of trust in the dynamite party. With the help of a gun from the drawer, he was perfectly capable of surprising Devlin and taking him in charge. Rossanna and McGee would be even less trouble. They could all take the place of Thackeray in the wood-store until police reinforcements arrived.

What held him back was the promise of something better:

the exposure and defeat of McGee's plan. Premature arrests would allow the Clan to assign the mission – whatever it was – to another group. No, there was always an optimum moment to swoop, and it was not yet.

The one thing gnawing at his conscience was the helplessness of Thackeray. If the torturing continued, he would certainly intervene. There was more than a possibility, though, that Devlin and Rossanna were now too occupied preparing for the visitors to expend more time trying to extract information from their stubborn prisoner.

Sensible as all this seemed, it left him with the task of building two infernal machines in little more than twenty-four hours. Why had Rossanna insisted upon two? Was one to be kept in reserve in case the first failed? He doubted it. The object of the demonstration was to make a strong and instantaneous impression on the emissaries from America. To admit that the first bomb had not exploded – and there would be a short delay while the second was rowed out and lowered into position in hope of more success – was unlikely to win anyone's confidence.

Surely it was likelier that the second bomb was wanted for some other target, perhaps in fulfilment of what Rossanna had termed 'the ultimate object of all our work'. If so, he had the opportunity of foiling the scheme by building one incapable of detonation. Marvellously straightforward – if only Rossanna had not insisted that her father would inspect both boxes when their contents were ready, and select the one to be used for the demonstration. Cribb's credibility depended on the success of the explosion by the lake.

The rest of that day and well into the afternoon of the

next was one of the most exacting and intensive periods of work he had ever set himself. As well as the dangerous task of assembling the bombs and making the infinitesimal adjustments that would decree success or failure, he had much to do at the lakeside, surveying the gazebo, rowing around its three sides and under the arched supports, calculating and preparing. Failure to destroy the building would be catastrophic, an admission of incompetence. In the merciless canon of the dynamite conspiracy, it warranted death.

At four o'clock he asked Devlin to inform Rossanna that the machines were ready. She came out to the lawn where, in the interests of safety, he had arranged the squat, black boxes.

'So here they are like two picnic-boxes!' she said. 'How much cold turkey did you put inside, Mr Sargent?'

'About twenty-five pounds in each, if I understand your meaning correct, Rossanna. I'm allowing for some resistance, you see.'

'It sounds a lot to me, but I'm sure you're the expert. Lift the lids, please, and show me the insides. Ah, how very neat! And both clocks ticking merrily away and keeping excellent time.'

'Nothing will be activated until the alarms are set,' said Cribb. 'But I don't advise anyone to touch the parts. It only wants the slightest pressure on a trigger . . .'

'I'm sure,' said Rossanna. 'Well, I shall save my congratulations for later. The visitors will be here at six o'clock. Father has decided that the destruction of the folly will take place exactly two hours after that. He wants you to remain out of sight until the smoke has cleared. Then you will appear, like Mephistopheles.'

'I hope it impresses 'em,' said Cribb with total sincerity. 'What are their names?'

'Mr Carse and Mr Millar. I have not met them myself. Father knows them, though. They are patriots like the rest of us, but they have the reputation of being hard-headed men. Now, gentlemen, if you would be good enough to go to the kitchen I think there is some ale there for you. While you are gone, I shall bring Father out to inspect the machines. He will wish to see them alone. Do not be concerned, Mr Sargent. I shall insist that he touches nothing. If you return in half an hour, I shall tell you which box is to be used tonight and you can activate the mechanism. Then we shall seal it, and you, Patrick, can help Mr Sargent convey it to the lake and deposit it as he directs.'

The first sign of the approach of spectators at the lake-side that evening was a flash of pale yellow through the trees, the shawl Rossanna was wearing, caught by the low-angled rays of the sun. They were using a more even path than the one she had led Cribb along on his first visit to the gazebo, probably because McGee was of the party. There were three bowler-hatted figures walking behind the chair.

Cribb picked up the field-glasses he had borrowed from the house, and looked for Carse and Millar. One of the bowlers was Devlin's, so he moved quickly on to the next. It was worn by a thick-set, grey-bearded man with florid skin and bulbous features. He was talking as he walked, using his clenched right fist to emphasize points.

Cribb shifted the focus to the second newcomer, who was speaking to no one, seeming content to stay remote

150

from the rest of the party. He stared fixedly ahead through thick, pebble-glass spectacles with wire frames. His height was not much over five feet and he had compensated for this by cultivating a large black moustache, bow-shaped so that the ends reached almost to the line of his jaw. For all the forceful gestures of the big man, this one conveyed more menace.

They stopped at the waterside, some eighty yards from the gazebo on the other side of the lake. It was fully two hours since Cribb and Devlin had lowered the box by ropes from the rowing-boat into the water. They had lodged it as closely as possible to the base of one of the arched supports. It had seemed to come to rest gently. Nothing inside the box should have been disturbed. They had not remained long in the vicinity after lowering the bomb, even so.

Cribb took out a silver watch Devlin had loaned him. Possibly it had belonged to Malone. It registered two minutes to eight. He flicked his tongue tensely across his upper lip and stared across the water at the gazebo. It looked depressingly solid in construction, its reflection giving the illusion that there was as much brickwork below the surface as above. Two crows were perched on the battlements. How humiliating if the explosion just dislodged a few bricks and failed to disturb the birds . . .

Feeling not at all like Mephistopheles, he started walking under cover of the trees towards the waiting group, ready to appear on cue. Those two minutes must have ticked away by now. At least, he wryly observed, the thing had not gone off *before* time.

He was near enough now to hear the murmur of conversation, and most of it seemed to be coming from the larger of the two emissaries, punctuated with the kind of laughter one hears filling the intervals at firework displays, when the set pieces are slow in igniting. The other, standing apart, had his watch in his hand and was concentrating all his attention on the gazebo.

Cribb had gone as close to the others as he could without revealing his presence. He stood behind a tree, took out the watch and lifted the cover. Three minutes past the hour. They were not going to wait much longer and nor was he. If he made a dash to the house now, he should be able to get to the kitchen and release Thackeray, and the two of them might get clear before the alarm was raised.

Even as he was reaching a decision, the leaves above him rustled and a boom of reassuring volume shattered the calm of the evening. Before doing anything else, he put back the hands of the watch to precisely eight o'clock.

The crows were two small specks in the sky when he turned round, but the gazebo was still disintegrating. It was collapsing into the water by layers with extraordinary slowness, like snow slipping off a roof. More than half was gone already and the lake's surface was fretted with waves radiating from the point of disturbance. The roof, deprived of support, slipped into the void, bringing more masonry with it and hitting the water with an impact that sent droplets showering down over much of the lake. When everything went still again, one section of one wall remained.

He walked towards the group. Rossanna, with arms outspread, seemed ready to embrace him, but took his hands instead and drew him towards the visitors. 'And here, gentlemen, is the genius behind what we have just witnessed. Mr Sargent, I want to introduce you to Mr Millar.'

The larger of the emissaries offered a broad hand to Cribb. 'You seem to have a way with the little cakes, Sargent. It was neatly done.'

'Mr Carse,' said Rossanna.

The small man remained where he was, holding his watch. 'Three and a half minutes late,' he said in an expressionless voice. 'I do not regard that as genius.'

Cribb's response was immediate. 'Late? It was perfectly on time. I checked it on the watch I was given.' He took it out. 'Why, it isn't three minutes past *yet.*'

'Then there would appear to be an error in the watch,' said Carse in the same flat voice. 'I suppose we cannot blame you for that if you set the bomb mechanism from the same instrument.'

'He did,' insisted Rossanna. 'It was done in my presence.'

'In future,' said Carse, 'we shall ensure that all time-pieces are accurately synchronized. I am sure your father concurs. Shall we return to the house, or are we to be treated to some other proof of Mr Sargent's genius?'

'Father thought that this would be sufficient,' said Rossanna. 'He is personally convinced of Mr Sargent's professional ability and he has made the most comprehensive inquiries into his background. He was hoping that we could enrol him as a member of the Clan this evening. Are you prepared to accept him, Mr Carse?'

'Since Malone is dead, madam, and your father incapacitated, we have no choice. Time is short. Bring your prodigy to the meeting and we shall conduct the usual ceremony.'

As Carse strode away along the path in the direction of the house, with Millar not far behind in company with Devlin, Rossanna hung back to speak to Cribb. 'There is something I must tell you. Pretend you are helping me with the wheelchair. This man Carse—'

'The leprechaun?'

'Do not underestimate him. He has been exceedingly difficult over the matter of Malone.'

'Nasty little cove.'

'He was incensed at what we had to tell him. He was ready to cancel everything – a year's work – until we told him about you. Even then, he was most disbelieving about your ability to stand in for Malone.'

'I rather formed that impression too,' said Cribb.

'We had to paint you in glowing colours. Upon one point, in particular I bent the truth a little.'

'What was that?'

'The senior members of the Clan are most particular about one of the rules regarding descent. Everyone presented for membership has to have the Irish blood, you see.'

'Now that's a problem,' said Cribb.

'It might have been. I told them your mother was born in Skibbereen and that silenced them.'

'It's silenced me,' said Cribb. 'Where the devil is it?'

'In County Cork. It's one of the southernmost towns in Ireland. Carse comes from Dublin, so it's unlikely that he knows Skibbereen. You don't mind the deception, do you?'

'I'll square it with my conscience somehow. One needs to bend the truth occasionally in my profession.'

She smiled her thanks. 'That was a darling of a demolition, Mr Sargent. We'll not waste your second bomb on a folly, I promise you. It'll be a deadly serious thing next time. If it does its work as well as the first, you'll be the toast of all Ireland. There should be no worry, for the machines are identical, are they not?'

'Like two peas from the same pod, Rossanna,' said Cribb, speaking the truth.

At the house, he was instructed to wait in the hall while certain preliminaries took place in the drawing room. After some fifteen minutes, Rossanna came out with a black mask, like the one her father wore, except that it had no eye-spaces. 'Do I have to wear that?' he asked.

'It's part of the ritual,' she explained, as she tied it firmly in place. 'But you will be perfectly safe. The ballot for your membership has taken place and you got no black balls. You will be among friends. I shall hold your arm to guide you.' She gave it a reassuring squeeze and led him forward.

He felt his feet leave the tiles and move on to carpet. The door closed behind him. A deep voice that he recognized as Millar's spoke close in front of his face. 'What is your name, friend?'

'Sargent.' There was no response to this, so he shrewdly added, 'Michael Sargent.'

'Very good. Tell us the names of your father and mother.'

He felt a slight pressure from Rossanna. 'John Sargent and Molly O'Doherty.' He paused for effect. 'Of Skibbereen, in County Cork.'

Someone near by grunted in satisfaction.

'My friend,' said Millar over a rustle of paper, suggesting that he was reading from a text, 'you have sought affiliation with us animated by love, duty and patriotism.'

'Not to say the Skirmishing Fund,' murmured a voice in the background, possibly Devlin's.

'Stow your jaw, mister!' said Millar, before continuing, in priestlike tones, 'We have deemed you worthy of our confidence and our friendship. You are now within these secret walls. Those who surround you have all taken the obligations of our Order, and are endeavouring to fulfil its duties. These duties must be cheerfully complied with, or not at all undertaken. We are Irishmen banded together for the purpose of freeing Ireland and elevating the position of the Irish race. The lamp of the bitter past plainly points our path, and we believe that the first step on the road to freedom is secrecy. Destitute of secrecy, defeat will again cloud our brightest hopes; and, believing this, we shall hesitate at no sacrifice to maintain it.'

Cribb felt a hand fasten on his shoulder.

'Be prepared, then, to cast aside with us every thought that may impede the growth of this holy feeling among Irishmen; for, once a member of this Order, you must stand by its watchwords of Secrecy, Obedience and Love. With this explanation, I ask you are you willing to proceed?'

'Answer,' whispered Rossanna.

'I am willing,' said Cribb.

'Approach the President, then,' ordered another voice. It belonged to Carse.

Rossanna piloted him in that direction.

'My friend,' said Carse, without a trace of affection, 'by your own voluntary act you are now before us. You have learned the nature of the cause in which we are engaged – a cause honourable to our manhood, and imposed upon us by every consideration of duty and patriotism. We would not have an unwilling member among us, and we give you, even now, the opportunity of withdrawing, if you so desire.'

Cribb thought it politic to shake his head at the suggestion.

Carse went on, 'Everyone here has taken a solemn and binding oath to be faithful to the trust we repose in him. This oath, I assure you, is one which does not conflict with any duty you owe to God, to your country, your neighbours, or yourself. It must be taken before you can be admitted to light and fellowship in our Order. With this assurance, will you submit yourself to our rules and regulations and take our obligation without mental reservation?'

'I will,' said Cribb. With an assurance like that, a man could promise anything.

'Place your right hand on this flag of free Ireland, then, and say after me . . .'

Cribb repeated the oath phrase by phrase, 'I, Michael Sargent, do solemnly and sincerely swear, in the presence of Almighty God, that I will labour, while life is left me' – (an inauspicious phrase, he thought) – 'to establish and defend a republican form of government in Ireland. That I will never reveal the secrets of this organization to any person or persons not entitled to know them. That I will obey and comply with the Constitution and laws of the United Brotherhood, and promptly and faithfully execute all constitutional orders coming to me from the proper authority, to the best of my ability. That I will foster a spirit of unity, nationality and brotherly love among the people of Ireland.

'I furthermore swear that I do not now belong to any other Irish revolutionary society antagonistic to this organization, and that I will not become a member of such society while connected with the Brotherhood, and, finally, I swear that I take this obligation without mental reservation, and that any violation hereof is infamous and merits the severest punishment. So help me God.'

Two loud raps followed.

'Brothers and Sister!' said Millar's voice. 'It affords me great pleasure to introduce you to our new brother.'

Another rap.

'Now take off your blindfold, Sargent, and let us get down to the serious business of the meeting,' said Carse.

12

Cribb blinked, accustoming his eyes to the gaslight. As he had estimated, the meeting was taking place in the drawing room. His newly acquired sister and brothers were ranged round him in a circle of high-backed chairs which included McGee's invalid-chair. Carse, the senior man present, wore a chain of office with a silver pendant in the shape of a shield. On it was engraved a harp, two sides of which formed the arched body and wing of an angel.

'Sit down, tenderfoot. We've finished with you,' Carse told him brusquely.

He found a place between Devlin and Rossanna.

'Now, Sister,' Carse continued, with a thin smile directed to Cribb's right. 'We shall be obliged if you will deliver your father's report on the work in hand.'

A familiar perfume was wafted Cribb's way as Rossanna stirred in her chair. A small pulse at the back of her neck was throbbing visibly. Cribb had the strong intimation that she regarded Carse and Millar as potential enemies. 'Well, gentlemen, the good news is that everything is ready. We have all been witnesses this evening to the devastation wreaked by Brother Sargent's machine. An explosive device of identical construction, clock-timed and watertight, is waiting to be put into use. It requires only to be activated.'

Carse nodded. 'That's all in order then. But what about the Holland project? The bomb's no use if that's not finished. You've had a year to put it together and God knows how many dollars to pay for it. Is it ready as your father promised?'

'Might I suggest that you come and see for yourselves?' said Rossanna. 'If it is possible for the meeting to adjourn for a few minutes, I have hurricane lamps ready and we can walk down to the workshop and ascertain whether the Clan's dollars have been wisely invested.'

'Very well,' said Carse. 'Collect your hats, Brothers.'

Outside, the moon was obscured by a bank of cloud, so the lamps were necessary at once. Devlin led, the others filing after him in silence, impressed, it seemed, with the solemnity of the occasion. With the addition of a couple of spades, Cribb reflected, they could have passed for an exhumation party.

They stopped at the door of the large building where Devlin's team had been employed. Devlin produced a ring of keys and unfastened two locks. The door opened inwards and they passed inside.

Cribb first noticed a strong smell of tar. Then he was compelled to turn his shoulders and move sideways along the inner side of the building. The farther he penetrated, the narrower the passage became. The building accommodated an object of such proportions that it was impossible in that confined area to estimate its shape. All he could tell in the uncertain light was that the section nearest him was curved and made of riveted metal plates coated with tar. It rose above the height of his bowler.

'Climb the step-ladder ahead of you, Mr Sargent, and you will get a better view,' Rossanna's voice advised him.

He found a ladder roped to part of the wooden framework that flanked the object. He climbed it and joined Devlin and Carse on a small platform, two planks in width. Devlin hooked his lamp on to one of the cross-beams above them, and Millar, who had appeared on a similar platform on the opposite side, did the same, so producing the best illumination possible in the circumstances. The shadow of Rossanna, climbing the ladder on Millar's side, danced to the swinging of the lamps.

Cribb still had difficulty in recognizing the object. Its main section was in the shape of a cigar about thirty feet long, and there was a low turret-shaped superstructure in the centre.

'There, gentlemen,' said Rossanna, 'you see the culmination of a year's work.'

'Nine years,' Carse corrected her. 'This was begun with John Holland's work in New Jersey.'

'Who is John Holland?' Cribb inquired, hopeful that the answer might explain the purpose of the metal cigar.

'Holland?' said Devlin, in a tone suggesting that the question should not have been asked. 'He is the fellow who has made the submarine boat a practical reality. An Irishman, born in County Clare, and a Fenian, thank God. He built his first with Fenian money as long ago as 1875, three years after he arrived in the States. The man has thought of nothing else but designing submarine boats since he was a boy in Liscannor. This is an improved version of the Holland III, known as the *Fenian Ram.*'

'It had better be improved,' said Carse. 'Sixty thousand dollars of the Skirmishing Fund went into the first three boats, for nothing more sensational than a few excursions up the Passaic River.'

'She has undergone two months of trials in the Estuary,' said Devlin. 'She is ready for whatever action is required of her. Would you care to see inside? There is a hinged lid, you see—'

'That can wait,' said Carse quickly. 'How is she powered? With an oil engine, like the *Ram*?'

'Oh, no,' said Devlin. 'This vessel is electrically driven. She has two Edison-Hopkinson motors capable of developing up to forty-five horse-powers. Each one is powered by an Elwell-Parker battery with fifty-two accumulators. They produce a tension of 104 volts.'

'It sounds capital,' said Millar from the other side, 'but as a man without much knowledge of electricity it doesn't mean a damned thing to me, Brother. What's her top speed below the surface, and how long can she stay under?'

'She'll do eight knots submerged,' said Devlin, 'and she could stay under indefinitely. It's the air the crew have to breathe that limits the length of the submersions.'

'Limits them to what?' asked Millar.

'I would estimate two hours with a crew of three.'

Millar and Carse exchanged glances. 'That should suffice,' said Carse. 'How deep can she dive with safety?'

Devlin tapped the hull of the submarine boat with his shoe. 'She's constructed of Siemens-Martin steel plates five-sixteenths of an inch thick. They'll withstand the pressure fifty feet down, if necessary. And she can hide in ten feet of water. I can give you a demonstration tomorrow.'

'That won't be possible,' said Carse. 'We shall have to take your word for it that everything is in order. But as you were selected for this assignment on account of your knowledge of Holland's work, we have every confidence in you, Brother.'

Rossanna spoke. 'If you have seen enough, gentlemen, shall we return to the house? There is still my father's plan to expound.'

They shortly resumed in the dining room, where a large chart of the river between Erith Reach and the Lower Hope was spread across the table. McGee, masked as usual, was seated at the head. At Rossanna's reappearance, he started babbling incoherently. She took his hand in hers and quietened him, but not before Millar had taken Cribb aside. 'Is he always like this?' he asked.

'It's a speech impediment,' said Cribb. 'The legacy of his accident.'

'Poor beggar! You wouldn't believe there's a brain still functioning behind that piece of silk.'

'It's hard to credit,' Cribb agreed.

'Come, Brothers, we have much to do,' Carse called from across the table. 'Sister McGee, we await your father's report.'

Rossanna was on her feet. 'Gentlemen, my father wishes to welcome you to this meeting of our camp, here in the enemy's country. A year has passed since he left his brothers in New York and set sail for England with the object of putting John Holland's work to practical use on this side of the Ocean. It has been a difficult year, blighted by adversity, but in all our work the flame of the cause has burned bright, never flickering, nor threatening to go out. Maimed as he is, crippled and bereft of speech, my father is still the revolutionary you commissioned to carry out the active work of the Clan. And he is proud to report that with the loyal support of other members of the group here present,

163

not to say the practical assistance of patriots domiciled in London, he has brought his work to perfection.'

'We shall form our own opinion about that,' said Carse, without much charity. 'What is the plan?'

Unperturbed, Rossanna continued: 'Well, gentlemen, I think you know. Our purpose is assassination. We are pledged to take the life of a certain personage, to demonstrate the strength and resolve of the Irish movement. The difficulties of such a mission at the present time are legion. There is not a public figure in London, not one miserable under-secretary, who does not have his personal bodyguard. You cannot get within a hundred yards of a public building with anything that distantly resembles an infernal machine.

'But the more difficult the task is made, the more brilliant will its achievement seem. We have been compelled to answer English organization with Irish genius. Our submarine boat gives us the means of penetrating the enemy's defences by a route they cannot dream is possible. For many months, our agents have observed the passage of sea-going ships up and down the reaches of the Thames. It was thought at first that we might mount an attack with torpedoes on one of the vessels of the merchant fleet. Then a more audacious plan suggested itself. It is the custom for ships to anchor in Gravesend Reach to wait for the next tide for the last mile upriver. Outgoing vessels, too, break their journeys here for at least one tide to take on passengers. Gravesend has become the place for fashionable people to embark and disembark. They pass between the ships and Gravesend pier on small steam-launches. Mr Gladstone himself used Gravesend after his cruise in the *Pembroke Castle* with the Tennysons and Sir Donald Currie last September.'

'Jesus! If only we'd been ready, we could have done for Gladstone!' said Devlin.

'And set the cause back twenty years,' said Carse witheringly. 'The Clan does not murder indiscriminately. Gladstone for all his faults provides the best hope we have of achieving Home Rule. Please go on, Sister.'

'I was remarking that Gravesend is patronized by all the most illustrious ocean-going travellers,' said Rossanna. 'It was obvious to my father that sooner or later some person suitable for assassination would appear there. But rather than focus our attention on the ship, and attack it with torpedoes, he fastened on a more certain means of destroying our victim; it is to attach a watertight box containing a bomb to the underside of the pier. It will be clock-timed, of course, and set according to the itinerary, which is always conveniently published in the newspapers when personages of that class set sail.'

'Stunning!' said Millar. 'The submarine boat can deposit the bomb two hours ahead, and be clear of the area by the time it detonates.'

'Exactly. And it is far more certain to account for its victim than a torpedo fired at the iron hull of a great ocean-going vessel.' Rossanna surveyed her audience to see that the point was taken.

Carse placed his hand palm downwards on the table. 'One moment. This pier. It would need to be a floating pier to take account of tidal variations, would it not?'

'Lord, yes,' said Devlin. 'The average rise and fall is fifteen feet. But the river is twenty-five feet deep at low water at Gravesend. We've been into all this.'

'I don't doubt that you have. What I cannot comprehend is how you propose to attach Brother Sargent's bomb to the underside of the pier. When you are ten feet under water in a submarine boat, you cannot open the man-hole in the roof, you know.'

Devlin ignored the sarcasm. 'That is why I have devised an apparatus – a form of harness – to convey the bomb on top of the conning-tower, after the fashion of the rack on top of a cab. Several hooks will project upwards ready to fasten on to the pier when we pass beneath it and so detach the bomb from its harness.'

Carse released a long breath, vibrating his lips at the same time. 'That sounds extremely hazardous to me.'

'Courting disaster,' added Millar, for emphasis.

'What if the mechanism of the bomb is disturbed?' said Carse.

Cribb decided some expert reassurance was wanted. 'Ah, if that happens, it's a guinea to a gooseberry that the thing won't detonate at all.'

'But Mr Sargent's bomb is so beautifully packed that it is most unlikely to be disturbed by the manoeuvre,' Rossanna quickly added. 'You must examine it yourselves. It's as neat as a picnic-hamper from Fortnum and Mason.'

Cribb noted the compliment. It was comforting to know that if he was drummed out of the Force for his part in these activities, there might be an opening in the grocery trade.

'Very well,' said Carse. 'Let us presume that the explosion is successful. What guarantee is there that it will destroy a man standing upon the pier?'

'I should have thought the answer to that was obvious,' said Rossanna, clearly becoming nettled by the trend of the conversation. 'This evening we saw a brick building totally demolished. We are now talking about a pier constructed of *wood*.'

The bulk of which,' countered Carse, 'is below the surface of the water. I think it would surprise you if you saw the volume of timber required to support a floating pier. The charge – if it detonates – will rend the planks asunder, I agree, but I am not so sure that it will kill anyone standing on top. We have not gone to so much trouble and expense to let our victim off with a ducking.'

'But the gazebo was blown to smithereens by a bomb ten feet underneath,' persisted Rossanna.

'Not so, my dear,' said Carse. 'Brother Sargent's bomb destroyed part of the understructure. When that was gone, the building collapsed. What we saw tonight was admirable in its way, but quite a different exercise from blowing up Gravesend pier.' He paused, before adding, with exaggerated courtesy, 'Sister.'

Rossanna flushed with annoyance. 'Then perhaps – Brother – you can suggest a better way of doing it.'

'Certainly,' said Carse in the same bland tone. 'How much dynamite do we have in store here, Brother Devlin?'

'About two hundredweight.'

'Very good. And is this submarine boat capable of conveying that amount to Gravesend?'

Devlin frowned, puzzled. 'I don't see why not.'

'Very well. This is my proposal, then. Instead of trying to do clever underwater tricks with hooks and harness, we make quite sure that our bomb is lodged in the right place by converting our submarine boat into the biggest and most devastating infernal machine in history. In other words, we stuff the boat with dynamite – including Brother Sargent's estimable bomb, which in these circumstances will serve as the detonator – and anchor it below the pier. When it explodes, the pier and everyone on it will be blown to bits, and probably half Gravesend as well.'

'Cripes, that's brilliant!' crowed Millar. 'It can't fail!'

'Destroy the submarine boat?' said Devlin, disbelievingly. 'It's taken a year to assemble it.'

'I appreciate your sentiments, Brother,' said Carse. 'It's a fine piece of engineering. But it was built for one occasion. This is not the kind of exercise one repeats at intervals. Once the job is done, we can never hope to take the British by surprise in the same way again. Far better that the thing is destroyed in action than allowed to survive for the river-police to track down in the intensive search they will certainly mount after the operation. This way is safer for us all.'

'I don't think that is altogether true.' Rossanna had spoken, her voice more controlled and deliberate than before.

'Why not?' demanded Carse.

'Because one of us at least will have to pilot the boat into position under the pier. How is that person going to escape?'

'That's a fact!' said Devlin. 'If the boat stays down there, someone has to be inside it.' Even as he spoke the words, their full implication dawned on him. His eyes bulged in horror. 'I'm the only one who knows how to pilot the thing!'

Carse raised his palm in restraint. 'Let us not sully the dignity of the meeting by effusions of panic, Brother. There is no reason why we should not conduct our discussion in a civilized fashion. One does not wish to be put into the position of blackballing another member of the Clan, but as Chairman I have my duty to do and I shall certainly not

168

shirk it, if free speech is threatened. I was about to come to the most interesting part of my proposal: the identity of our candidate for assassination.' He paused dramatically. 'At this moment there is an ocean-going yacht, the *Hildegarde*, moored in Gravesend Reach. Tomorrow morning at half past ten, as the tide turns, it is due to set sail on a ten-day cruise through the Straits of Dover and along the south coast. All of the party but one are already aboard. They include Lord Charles Beresford, Sir Charles Dilke and several young women well known upon the London stage.'

'Moses!' ejaculated Cribb, unable to restrain himself. 'Would one of them by any chance be Mrs Lillie Langtry?'

Carse produced his approximation of a smile. 'No, sir. Mrs Langtry is at present on tour in America. But I gather from your inquiry that you have my drift. The final member of the party is due to go aboard the *Hildegarde* tomorrow morning. He will arrive at Gravesend pier at ten o'clock, having come by landau from Marlborough House.'

'The Prince of Wales?' said Devlin, half in horror.

'Albert Edward, the heir to the throne of England,' said Carse. '"Bertie" to his friends, "Tum-Tum", one is told, to his intimates. He is to be our victim.'

'Magnificent!' declared Millar.

'A suitable sacrifice to the cause of republicanism,' said Carse. 'And justification for all our efforts. Perhaps you can now understand why there must be no possibility of failure. We *must* blow up the submarine and the pier with it.'

There was silence. Everyone was stunned by the enormity of what had been suggested.

After an interval, Rossanna said, 'I should like to consult my father.' She took McGee's hands and engaged in what appeared to be an intensive bout of finger-talk. 'Father praises the audacity of the plan,' she presently told Carse, 'but he still wishes to know how you propose to get the submarine boat into position.'

Carse nodded. 'A reasonable inquiry. First, I shall put a question to Brother Devlin. I believe, sir, that you have piloted the boat on all its trials so far. Is that true?'

'Yes,' Devlin gloomily agreed.

'And has anyone else accompanied you?'

'The late Brother Malone, rest his soul,' said Devlin. 'And Miss McGee, and her father, on different occasions.'

'Good. And is it a difficult manoeuvre to cause the submarine boat to dive and travel underwater to a stated destination?'

'If you could see clearly underwater, it would be child's play,' said Devlin. 'The mechanics are perfectly simple. But the Thames is full of impurities, as you know, so we have to steer by coming to the surface at intervals. It's a process known as "porpoising".'

'How appropriate! But the mechanics, you say, are simple. Once you had got within sight of the pier by means of porpoising, you could hand the wheel with confidence to any one of us for the last submersion – first leaving the boat yourself and swimming to a convenient launch – is that so?'

The persecuted look lifted miraculously from Devlin's face. 'Why, yes! Anyone could take the boat for the last few yards.'

'Thank you,' said Carse, with the air of a barrister who has elicited a vital piece of information from a witness. 'And now I should like to put a point to all present. It is this: do you agree that the arrival of the Prince of

170

Wales tomorrow morning on Gravesend pier presents Ireland with an opportunity unparalleled in its history?'

'Jesus, yes!' said Millar, leading the chorus of assent.

'In that case, then,' said Carse, allowing a little emotion to enter his voice, 'is it too much to ask that one of you should volunteer to steer that submarine boat to its place below the pier, and so join the ranks of those who have laid down their lives for Ireland?'

'The martyrs,' said Millar with reverence. 'Wolfe Tone, Thomas Russell, Robert Emmet—'

'Stow it!' said Carse irritably. He looked hopefully round the table, but nobody was volunteering yet to swell the ranks of the martyrs. 'It seems to me,' he went on, 'that this is an opportunity that might be seized by a patriot whose life in recent years has been wholly dedicated to the fulfilment of such a moment of history. I refer, Sister McGee, to your father.'

'No!' said Rossanna emphatically.

'I should prefer to hear from Brother McGee himself,' said Carse. 'Nobody appreciates more than I the courage of our brother in carrying through his mission in spite of his appalling injuries. Would he see it fail at this stage for want of somebody to lay down his life for Ireland?'

'He has suffered enough!' protested Rosanna, on her feet.

'With his injuries, Sister, he will have nothing to live for when this work is done.'

'You can't ask him!' shouted Rossanna defiantly. 'I shan't tell you his answer! You can't make me!'

Carse turned to Millar. 'Take hold of this hysterical woman and eject her from the meeting. We shall obtain Brother McGee's answer without her.'

'No!' screamed Rossanna. 'Keep away from me!' She gripped the edge of the table.

Millar moved quickly and with a notable lack of gallantry. Before Rossanna had a chance to turn from the table he was behind her. He gripped the open collar of her dress at each side of her neck and wrenched the bodice apart, pulling the sides down over her shoulders to pinion her arms. Then he fastened his left hand over her mouth to silence her screams. A second later, he screamed himself and jerked it away, dripping blood where her teeth had punctured his flesh. In fury, he raised his clenched right fist above his shoulder to strike her down, but found it grasped and held by the person he knew as Sargent. 'What the bloody hell—?' he shouted.

'Steady now!' said Cribb. 'We want no violence, Brother.'

'He's right,' said Carse. 'Sit down, Millar. Leave it to him.'

Millar resumed his seat, clutching his wounded hand, leaving Cribb to face the wild-eyed Rossanna, her hands ready like claws to make their mark on anyone who came too close. The shreds of her bodice hung about her arms, leaving gaping areas of camisole and stays, which added to the general savagery of the spectacle.

'Will you come outside, Rossanna?' asked Cribb, as mildly as if they were both at a ball.

'Not while Father remains here.'

'In that case I must . . .' He dived boldly forward in mid-conversation, burying his right shoulder into the folds of her skirt and clasping both arms around her thighs below the bustle, in the approved fireman's rescue position. She toppled forward with the impact and he lifted her clean off the ground on his shoulder. '. . . remove you forcibly, Rossanna,' he said.

172

'Neatly done, Brother!' said Carse. 'Take her to her room and see that she gives us no more trouble.'

With Rossanna's fists raining blows on the lower regions of his back, Cribb carried her from the room. He mounted the stairs with difficulty, thankful when she seemed to regard her struggle as hopeless and gave up pummelling. In her room, he stood by the bed and spoke to her before putting her down. 'Now, Rossanna, I want you to believe that I shan't let your father be killed. Carse and Millar are dangerous men and we must let them think they are having things their way. When the time is right, we'll foil them, but you must help me.' He put her gently down on the bed. She lay passively, breathing heavily. 'I must tie you to the bed,' said Cribb, 'to make it seem convincing. Take off your stockings, please. I'll use those.'

To his profound relief, she compliantly drew off two lengths of black silk and handed them to him.

'Put your hands against the bars at the head of the bed.' He tied them securely, one stocking for each hand. Then he picked up the shawl she had worn earlier and bound it round her ankles. As an afterthought, he straightened the tatters of her dress to cover her shoulders. She nodded her thanks. 'Now I must get back to them,' he told her. 'Whatever happens, Rossanna, whatever they tell you, believe me I shall see that your father does not die in that submarine boat.'

'I believe you.'

Downstairs, Carse greeted him as he entered the dining room. 'Good work, Brother. You managed her in fine style. She'll thank you for it later, when she's had time to think it over. Women appreciate a firm hand. And now you may congratulate Brother McGee on his decision. We put my suggestion to him and he unmistakably nodded his head.'

'No doubt about it,' Millar confirmed.

'He will pilot the submarine boat on its last stage tomorrow morning,' continued Carse. 'Oh, and he will not be alone. I believe Miss McGee told you about the policeman being held prisoner in the house, who was brought here after his suspicious attempts to befriend Malone. He will accompany Brother McGee, tied up, of course, and heavily drugged. It will be a convenient way of disposing of him.'

Cribb's eyes widened. 'But we don't *know* that he's a policeman. We can't condemn a man to death simply because he bought a drink for one of us in a pub!'

'Oh, I wouldn't concern yourself about that,' said Carse. 'After all, the Prince of Wales hasn't bought drinks for any of us and *he's* marked down for destruction.'

13

Cribb's acquaintance with the criminal classes was not slight or superficial. Of the seven people in his life he could claim to have understood almost totally, five had been murderers. This was no discredit to Mrs Cribb and Thackeray (who were the other two); it was from professional necessity. However guilty a man appeared according to circumstantial evidence, it was not enough to justify a prosecution. You had to find the motive. So time and again he had sat with prisoners and stranglers, patiently taking the measure of their minds. And to a lesser degree, scores more of the law-breaking fraternity had come under his scrutiny, from blackmailers and swindlers to the petty criminals whose activities were dignified by the cant of the underworld – broadsmen, dippers, dragsmen, maltoolers, screevers and shofulmen. Not one in all his recollection was quite so odious as Carse.

Millar, of course, had just exhibited the violence. He would certainly have beaten Rossanna insensible if Cribb had not intervened. And if he had been left to carry her upstairs, the consequences were loathsome to imagine. Yet it was Carse who made the flesh creep most. His form of violence was more detestable because it was calculated to the last detail and unaccompanied by any emotion. He had condemned three men to death as coolly as if he were ordering a new suit. All that mattered to him was the neatness of the design.

And what a design! Attacks on royalty were nothing new; the Queen herself had survived eight separate attempts on her life, but they were all ineptly carried out, thank Heaven. Since the latest, two years ago at Windsor, and the recent dynamite scares, her personal bodyguard had been trebled, and her appearances in public practically abandoned. The Prince, too, never moved these days without two or three detectives at his shoulder. His presence at Gravesend tomorrow would be the occasion for a massive show of strength by the local police. No one on the route would be allowed within yards of the Royal carriage. The pier and riverside would be cleared of unauthorized persons. Thames Division would patrol Gravesend Reach and escort the launch carrying the Prince from the pier to the *Hildegarde*.

Who would suspect that assassins would strike from twenty feet below the pier?

Now that he knew the atrocity being planned, Cribb was in an appalling situation. The path of duty plainly lay in the direction of the nearest village. If the alarm were raised, the Prince could be persuaded to cancel tomorrow's arrangement. But once Cribb left the house, the dynamiters would realize they had been tricked. They would escape. And they would certainly kill Thackeray before they left.

He decided to stay. He was under no illusion; in making this decision he was accepting personal responsibility for the future King of England. But while there was a chance of saving Edward Thackeray of Rotherhithe as well as Albert Edward of the House of Saxe-Coburg, he was determined to take it. He would stake everything on his own ability to outwit Carse and Millar. There was already a plan in his mind.

At half past ten, he returned by arrangement to the dining room. Carse and Millar were there with McGee. On the table was the box containing the twin of the infernal machine that had gone under the gazebo. The lid was open.

'We were admiring your handiwork, Brother,' said Carse. 'So neatly put together! I believe this is identical with the first bomb. Is that so?'

'Absolutely,' said Cribb candidly. 'I was asked to make two bombs for Mr McGee to choose from. They were alike in every respect.'

'Good. Then we should have no disappointments tomorrow morning. Do you know, I cannot abide failure, Brother Sargent? If things go wrong I have the most queer compulsion to take revenge on those responsible. The results are sometimes unspeakably distressing. Are you ready to activate the machine? We shall want it to detonate at precisely five minutes past ten tomorrow. By then His Royal Highness will have shaken hands with the local dignitaries and be moving sedately along the pier to the waiting launch. Our agents have studied this procedure before.'

Cribb approached the box and carefully tilted the alarm clock so that its face was visible. Under the watchful eyes of the others it was quite impractical to move the alarm-hand to any position but the one Carse had indicated. 'Shall I set the clock to the correct time?' he asked.

Carse drew out a gold watch. 'Very well. But we shall take the time on my watch as the standard. Yours is incorrect by several minutes, if you remember. Set the hands to twenty minutes to eleven, taking care that the hour hand does not pass over the alarum hand.'

Cribb obeyed.

'Now you may wind the clock,' said Carse.

A lively ticking presently issued from the metal box.

'It's going all right,' said Cribb superfluously.

'But not activated yet, I think,' said Carse. 'You have still to wind the alarum. I believe it is the winder itself that makes contact with the trigger of the gun, is it not?'

'Yes, I was leaving that till last. Now that the times are set, I can put the clock face down and turn the winder, as you say. One needs to be careful at this stage.'

He completed the process, leaving the handle of the alarum in a position where it would strike the trigger with sufficient force to operate the firing-mechanism of the gun.

'Done!' said Cribb.

Carse turned to McGee. 'Is it in order?'

The hooded head nodded assent.

'Then I shall seal it, and you and I shall carry it ourselves to the submarine boat, Brother Millar. Thank you, Sargent. You will oblige us now by taking Brother McGee upstairs, with the servant's assistance. He is waiting in the hall, I believe.'

With a nod, Cribb took the handle of the wheel-chair and steered McGee out of the room. In the hall, the man-servant came to meet him. Together, they carried the chair upstairs. McGee was pathetically light in weight. At the bedroom door, the servant indicated that he could put McGee to bed without help. Cribb passed along the corridor and quietly let himself into Rossanna's room.

It would not have been wise to light the gas. He glided through the darkness until his knees came into contact with the bed. He whispered, 'Rossanna. It's me – Sargent. I'm going to untie you.'

She stirred, and he realized how close they were to each other. She murmured, 'Michael.'

It was the name he had invented for his oath-taking. He had practically forgotten.

He sat on the edge of the bed and felt for her left arm. The knot that bound her wrist had tightened, but a few seconds' work with his fingers succeeded in loosening it. He massaged her hand gently to restore the circulation, and then applied himself to the other knot, which held her right arm against the bars of the bedstead. This was more difficult, for it involved leaning across her body, but by hooking his right foot around the leg of the bed he contrived to maintain his balance while he worked at the knot. If he *did* come into contact with her person, it was the merest accidental touch of shirt and bodice and should not have prompted what happened next. The instant her right hand was released it snaked around his neck and pulled him firmly down towards the pillow. His right leg, still lodged behind the leg of the bed, contracted agonizingly. 'It is a year since these lips touched another's,' Rossanna whispered passionately. She guided his face towards hers just as his foot regained its liberty. With a small groan of relief, he let his weight bear downwards and felt his mouth meet hers, partly open and returning the pressure he involuntarily exerted.

In cataloguing the various holds that can immobilize a man, manuals of self-defence without exception neglect to state that pressure on the nape of the neck by a determined woman in a horizontal embrace is almost impossible to withstand. Several seconds passed before Cribb was able to draw back from Rossanna. Then she said, 'I shall not wait another year. That was exquisite, Michael Sargent, you impulsive man.'

Cribb, meanwhile, had retreated out of arm's range.

'Are you going to untie my ankles now?' inquired Rossanna.

'In a few minutes,' said Cribb warily. 'Keep your voice down. The servant is next door, attending to your father.'

'What has been going on downstairs?'

'They made me activate the bomb.'

She sat up in bed. 'The second bomb you made? Did you—'

'I had no choice,' said Cribb. 'They stood over me like prison warders. The clock is set for five past ten tomorrow morning. They've sealed the box and put it in the submarine boat. Devlin is packing the hull with all the dynamite left in the house.'

'Then nothing can be done,' said Rossanna. 'And you *promised* me that Father would not die.'

'I meant it. But first you must tell me the truth about him. Otherwise I can't help him.'

'What do you mean – the truth?'

'The real extent of his injuries,' said Cribb. 'All this deaf and dumb talk between you is play-acting, isn't it? He can't communicate a word to you.'

'What makes you say that?'

'Listen, my dear, I'm sure of it. That night when somebody broke in downstairs, I came into your bedroom here, but found it empty. I got out through your father's room, because I thought you might scream if you returned here and found me unexpectedly. And as I passed through, he watched me. His eyes followed me across the room. Next morning, over breakfast, you told us about the agitated state he was in for three-quarters of an hour after the disturbance, but you didn't say *why*. You had your suspicions, but you couldn't be sure, because he hadn't told you. Even when we were alone, taking our walk through the woods, it took a tumble in the bracken to convince you it was me. I remember the words you used: "Then you *did* come to my room last night." You mentioned hearing the floorboards upstairs creak as I returned to my room. If your father had been able to make you understand, Rossanna, you wouldn't have needed creaking floorboards to tell you who your visitor had been.'

Rossanna released a long breath. 'Very well, Michael. You're a perspicacious man. I shall speak the truth. His injuries are far more serious than anyone but me has realized. His brain was irretrievably damaged in the accident. He cannot talk or communicate except nod and shake his head. He is like a child, capable of performing simple instructions, but he has lost the power of independent thought.'

'And have you kept this from the others?'

'I believe so. Certainly no one in America knew the helplessness of his condition. When I was summoned here after the accident, I was not only shocked beyond words by his injuries, I was frightened, Michael, terrified. You don't know the Clan as I do. If they knew his brain was damaged, they would kill him. He has too many of their secrets. What use would it be to plead that he was helpless? And even if by some miracle they spared him, what future could there be? He was my provider, all that I had in the world. We should both be in the poor-house in a matter of weeks.'

'So you decided to create the impression that he was still able to lead the dynamite party?'

'What else could I do?' said Rossanna. 'I went through his papers and learned about the submarine boat that was to be constructed here. I found letters informing him that Tom Malone and Pat Devlin were sailing from New York with the Gaelic American Athletic Club, and would report here on arrival. They were bringing money, English sterling, enough to finance us for a year. I sent a transAtlantic cable in my father's name, informing the Revolutionary Directory of his accident and stating that he had lost the use of his legs and the power of speech, but was otherwise unimpaired. With my help – and I knew that I was listed by the Clan as a patriot and a member of the Ladies' Land League – he would carry on the work. It was confirmed by return that the arrangement was acceptable to New York. When Tom and Pat arrived I showed the cablegram to them, and they accepted me without question.'

'Did you intend to carry out the plot exactly as your father had projected it?'

'I did – until this evening. The only departure from his plan was that you replaced Tom Malone. How was Father to know New York would send us a man who panicked at the first whiff of danger? You can't have a dynamiter with a nervous disposition – it's a contradiction in terms. He would have killed us all sooner or later. I did the only thing I could. It's still our secret, isn't it?' She stretched her hand forward and gripped his arm.

'I didn't see what happened,' said Cribb. 'Merely heard a shot, didn't I?'

'You're a trump, Michael Sargent, a veritable trump, as

I live and breathe!' She tugged him determinedly towards her.

'I'm sure you do, Rossanna,' said Cribb, arresting the movement just as a strand of her hair feathered the tip of his nose. 'But there are things I have to be clear about if I'm to help your father tomorrow. Is he capable of controlling the submarine boat?'

'I believe he is,' said Rossanna. 'Patrick has always maintained that it is the simplest boat in the world to pilot, and of course they don't expect Father to take the wheel until Gravesend pier is in sight. As I told you, he will carry out any simple instruction you give him. He is pleased to do things, like a small child. That's why all this is so unfair. He doesn't understand that they have persuaded him to commit suicide. What can you do to stop it, Michael?'

'Leave it to me. Be on your guard tomorrow. They're likely to take you with them, to interpret anything he might wish to say. But don't imagine you can defeat them. Trust me – however black things seem.'

'Very well, Michael. One thing baffles me, though. You are a professional adventurer, yet here you are siding with those who are in no position to reward you. Carse and Millar are the paymasters. By interfering with their plans, you sacrifice the fee they would have paid you.'

It was the sort of devastatingly practical remark women were liable to slip into a conversation when you least expected it.

'Perhaps money isn't my only consideration,' suggested Cribb, lost for a convincing explanation.

To his immense surprise, Rossanna seized his shoulders and planted another emphatic kiss on his lips. Her hour or so strapped to the bed seemed to have left her in a demonstrative frame of mind. 'That was beautiful to hear,' she told him.

He extricated himself with difficulty and got to his feet. 'Time I was gone, Rossanna,' he said. 'Much more to do tomorrow.' It was only after he had crossed the room, gone through the door and closed it behind him that he remembered her legs were still tied together. He did not go back.

Instead, he went downstairs and out into the garden. Although it was late, the warmth of the day still lingered in the air. From farther down towards the river came voices, Devlin's for sure, and Millar's. The occasional metallic thump suggested they were working on the submarine boat, possibly moving the dynamite about the hull, with the intention of spreading the ballast as evenly as possible. He could not distinguish words in the conversation, but from the rising and falling tones it was clear that whatever they were doing required frequent consultation. All the signs were that the work would occupy them for some time yet.

One vital part of Cribb's plan needed to be attended to before the morning: he had to visit Thackeray and prepare him for the ordeal to come. His reasons for taking such a risk were not wholly compassionate; his poor, benighted assistant was entitled to be told the fate the Clan had decreed for him, but the paramount reason for seeing him was to warn him not to take food or drink in the morning, for it would certainly be drugged. If the counter-plan was to have any chance at all, Thackeray would need not only to be conscious, but capable of action. Until this moment, Cribb had intended going to him by night, as he had on the last occasion, but the sounds from Devlin's workshop made him change his mind. Now, when such preoccupying things were going on outside, was a better time than the small hours for moving secretly about the house.

He re-entered the building through the conservatory and crossed the hall to the dining room. At the kitchen door he paused, listening, in case the servant was inside. Most domestics, being early risers, liked to get to bed tolerably early, but this was an exceptional night in this household. One could take nothing for granted. Hearing no sound, though, he entered and found it in darkness. He crossed to the scullery and opened the door. The cat, again, was the solitary occupant. It treated him like a favourite table, pressing itself against his legs. He carefully slipped the bolts on the door of Thackeray's prison and opened it.

'Thackeray?' In the darkness, it was difficult to distinguish the figure on the bed of sacks. He took a step closer, and discovered nobody was there.

Thackeray had been moved.

'Gone!' said a voice close to his ear. He knew from the flat, almost bored tone that it was Carse. 'It would be wise not to move. The pressure you can feel in the small of your back is from a revolver.' He must have been standing there in the darkness behind the door, waiting for this.

'Brother Carse?' said Cribb, trying to gain time to think. Infuriating to step into a trap like this!

'Not your brother any longer,' said Carse. 'You've shown me what you really are – Copper. Lie down on those sacks, and don't make the mistake of thinking I can't see you. I've been waiting here for you for twenty minutes, so my eyes are quite accustomed to the dark.'

'Waiting for me?' repeated Cribb, struggling to understand where he had gone wrong.

'Do as I say,' said Carse, more in the manner of a suggestion than an order, 'or I shall be obliged to put a bullet in your back. It achieves the same result, but I really wouldn't wish to raise the entire household at this late hour by discharging a gun.'

Cribb groped down towards the sacks. Carse was right: in these conditions it would be suicidal to resist. A man deprived of sight is no match for two functioning eyes and a gun.

'Would you like to know your mistake?' Carse was still a disembodied voice, and the removal of the gun from Cribb's back was no comfort at all. It was probably pointing at his head. Was this to be the last conversation of his life?

He decided to prolong it. 'I'm interested, yes.'

'Naturally, I suspected you from the moment I heard about your appearance here. It was just too timely to be acceptable. Things do not happen in such a convenient way, but McGee and the others were so beset with difficulties that they wanted to believe what they should have questioned and rejected. And I give you credit – you have been well primed. Can you see me yet? The gun is aimed at the point between your eyes. Yes, your skill as a machinist is remarkable for a guardian of the law. The demonstration at the lake tonight all but convinced me you were really a professional.'

'What was wrong, then?' ventured Cribb, nurturing the conversation with painstaking care.

'Your mistake?' said Carse. 'That was later. I set a small trap for you. I suspected, you see, that this man who was captive here – Thackeray, I think you called him just now – was one of the police, although no amount of questioning or persuasion had tempted him to admit the fact. And I also reasoned that if *you* were a policeman, you would by now have located Thackeray and communicated with him. From the account I had from Devlin and Miss McGee of the disturbance the other night, it seemed highly probable that you were thus engaged when they suspected someone had broken in. It seemed likely to me that Thackeray would have told you about his interrogations, and triumphantly reported that he had not divulged his connection with the police. So tonight, after you returned from so capably subduing Miss McGee, I tested you in two ways. I stated, quite unequivocally, that our prisoner was a police officer. And you, correctly, reminded us that we did not *know* such a thing. This, of course, told me for certain that you had talked to Thackeray; otherwise you would not have known our interrogations had been unsuccessful.'

'I see,' said Cribb. 'What was the other test you gave me?'

'Ah, that was simply to inform you of our plan to send Thackeray to destruction in the submarine boat. It practically ensured that you would make an attempt to release him tonight – and what better time than when everyone appeared to be occupied in the boat-house? I simply transferred Thackeray to the dynamite store and settled down here to wait for you. You were not long in coming.'

'Now that I've fulfilled your expectations,' said Cribb, 'what are you going to do with me?'

'I could blow your brains out now, couldn't I?' said Carse. 'As it happens, though, I have a well-developed sense of irony. I rather enjoy the notion of Scotland Yard sending two men to insinuate themselves into the dynamite party, and training one of them so efficiently in the art of bomb-making that he prepares the charge that blows the Prince of Wales to Kingdom-come. Not only that; there is the added piquancy of our two gallant protectors of the realm actually manning the diabolical underwater machine that does the deed. You will accompany Thackeray and McGee tomorrow morning. It really is a pity. There are unlikely to be enough recognizable pieces of any of you left for the authorities to appreciate the full irony of what has happened, but I shall enjoy it.'

14

A white mist hung low over the river at 6 a.m. next morning when Cribb was marched down the path leading to the landing-stage. His wrists were lashed behind his back with thick cord, drawn so tight by Millar that all sensation had gone from his hands. Two broad belts pinioned him, one at the level of his chest, the other his waist. They, too, had been tightened to the maximum. Millar had crushed his boot against Cribb's back with the zeal of the head of a family fixing straps round the holiday portmanteau. The constriction complicated breathing: he had to take repeated short, shallow breaths; anything deeper was insufferably painful.

Ahead, the steam-launch was moored at the landing-stage. Beyond, loomed the whale-like outline of the submarine boat, lying low in the water, the small conning-tower forming no more than a hump on its back.

'Step aboard,' called Carse from the cabin of the launch. 'And be quick about it. We must make Gravesend by eight o'clock whatever happens, and this mist threatens to be difficult.'

In response to a push from Millar, Cribb stumbled aboard. Rossanna, deathly pale in a black cloak and hood, took his arm and guided him past a case of dynamite into the cabin. He felt most unlike the Paladin he had claimed to be the evening before, but he tried to summon a reassuring expression. If anything was to be salvaged from the ruins of his plan, it would require her co-operation.

'Cast off, then,' ordered Carse, who was at the wheel.

Millar obeyed, and the engine throbbed into life.

'We're going ahead,' Carse explained. 'Devlin will steer a similar course from behind. It's difficult enough trying to see through the scuttles in that thing, without contending with these conditions. Still, if the mist holds as far as Gravesend, he'll be able to approach much closer to the pier than we planned.'

'A river mist often lifts quite quickly as the sun comes up,' said Cribb.

'Stow your gammon, Copper,' growled Millar. 'You're a dead man. Have the decency to behave like one.'

The launch chugged steadily out into deeper water, with the black hull of the submarine boat settling in its wake. Occasionally a distant ship's siren sounded, but otherwise they were detached from the world. Visibility was variable, never more than fifty yards. Once they glimpsed a massive sailing-vessel, moored on the starboard side.

'The *Frederick William*,' Carse told them. 'A cadet-ship. Devlin told me to look out for her. We're passing Ingress Abbey, in that case. This will be one of the quietest stretches of the river. Marshes on either side. Are the others still in sight of us?'

'Close behind,' Millar confirmed. He chuckled softly.

'What's amusing you?' asked Carse.

'I was thinking it's a good thing Devlin ain't great shakes as a conversationalist, because he won't be getting much response from his passengers, McGee being dumb and Thackeray out to the world.'

They cruised on through Fiddler's Reach and made the steep turn into Northfleet Hope, pressing against the flood tide at little more than four knots. 'The steamboat jetty at Northfleet is the next landmark,' said Carse. 'I'll move in close so that we don't miss it. Soon after that we'll stop the engines and let Devlin draw alongside to take the copper aboard. I never did find out your name, did I?'

'Sargent will do,' said Cribb.

'Well then, Sargent, you'd better consider whether there's a last message we can pass to Scotland Yard on your behalf. You'll be taking your leave of us in a few minutes.'

'That looks like the jetty,' said Millar.

'Yes, that's it. And that will be the entrance to Northfleet dockyard,' said Carse. 'Any last words, Mr Sargent?'

As Cribb replied, he looked directly across the cabin at Rossanna. 'I've made my arrangements, thank you.' Silently, he mouthed the words he had spoken in her room the night before, 'Trust me.'

She nodded, unseen by Millar, who was peering through the mist for the first sighting of Gravesend.

'Please yourself,' said Carse. 'We've tried to do our best for you. Not every unsuccessful police spy gets a coffin made of Siemens-Martin steel, subscribed by Irish patriots. I'm shutting down the engines now, Millar. Signal Devlin to heave to alongside us, will you?'

The monstrous vessel sidled close to the launch, and presently the lid of the conning-tower opened and Devlin's head appeared.

'I think this will do,' Carse called up to him. 'How is she performing?'

'She's a capital craft,' said Devlin.

'Will you need more ballast when she submerges? I've got half a crate more of dynamite here on deck, ready to transfer if you need it.'

'That won't be necessary,' said Devlin. 'Let's get Sargent aboard.' He lifted a short metal ladder from inside the conning-tower and attached it to the side.

Cribb felt a prod in the back from Millar. 'Move up the ladder, Copper. Lean well forward and you shouldn't fall.'

Aided by several timely shoves from behind, Cribb negotiated the rungs. At the top, Devlin had emerged from the conning-tower. He grasped Cribb's shoulders as firmly as a throwing-hammer, summoned his strength with an emphatic grunt, and tipped him head first into the hatch. Like a hundredweight of coal, Cribb plunged towards the impact that promised to shatter his skull. By the fortune that only ever favoured him *in extremis*, he hit the side of an upholstered seat provided for the pilot. The rest of his body slumped painfully into a space between this and the steering mechanism.

'Get to the aft end, with your mate,' Devlin called, as he dropped down after him, and aimed a kick at his ribs. Cribb squirmed out of range, past the small, hunched figure of McGee, propped against a crate of dynamite. The interior was well-lit by two electric light bulbs. He recognized Thackeray's recumbent form and wedged himself beside it. The constable was breathing through his open mouth. With each exhalation the top layer of whiskers on his beard flattened like grass on a railway embankment. It would be quite some time before he regained his senses. There was no hope of help from that quarter for hours to come.

'He's well dosed with chloral,' Devlin said, clambering after Cribb. 'I've taken the precaution of binding his hands and feet, in case he wakes up before five past ten. And now I'm going to put a cord round your ankles and tether them to this stanchion, so that you don't disturb McGee. You can shout as much as you like, though, because he's stone deaf.'

Cribb felt the cord bite into his shins. Devlin's technique of fettering a man matched his strength. It would be impossible to escape without assistance.

'In case you wondered where the bomb is located,' said Devlin, 'I fitted it under the engine, by removing one of the steel plates and then riveting it back. There's no way of reaching your infernal machine from inside, Brother Sargent. Of course, you may move the dynamite about as much as you like if you succeed in getting free, but nothing you do in here can prevent this boat from being blown into a million pieces when the time comes.' He took out his watch. 'Lord, it's almost eight o'clock already. Time I gave McGee his instructions.' He returned to the front of the boat, picked up the crippled man from the deck with ease, and positioned him on the pilot's seat. Then, standing where McGee could follow the movements of his lips, he slowly identified the controls. 'Wheel. Starting switch. Levers to admit the water-ballast, to put the boat in diving trim. This switch controls the force-pump which ejects the water from the ballast chambers . . .'

Cribb listened keenly as the entire process was twice repeated. From where he was, it was difficult to see any of the controls, or how McGee was responding to the lesson.

'Now, it is quite straightforward,' Devlin insisted, articulating each word separately to assist comprehension,

'I shall start the engine and you need not switch it off until the boat is in position under the pier. To set the propellers in motion pull this handle towards you. You will then be under way. To submerge, push down the ballast-levers here and here . . .' By degrees, the instruction took a simpler turn. 'Now remember, this one to move forward. These, to go down. This to come up again. This for speed. And this to stop. The pier is two hundred yards ahead, so you will need to surface more than once. You will see the flags ahead. Do you understand? Very well. Now it is time to practise.'

The engine stuttered into life, sending painful vibrations through those parts of Cribb's body which still retained some feeling.

'Open the ballast chambers,' ordered Devlin. 'Excellent. Now we are in diving trim. Take her slowly forward.'

He took McGee systematically through the manoeuvres required to steer the boat to its position below the pier. As it submerged completely for the first time, Cribb dimly registered that the experience lacked the charm of taking to the air in a balloon, but he was frankly more occupied with devising some means of escape than savouring a new sensation. He nudged Thackeray sharply with his heels. There was still not the faintest response in the somnolent features.

'Splendidly done! You'll cope without any trouble at all,' Devlin announced from the controls. 'It's time I left you. I must call up the launch. Once I've closed the lid on the conning-tower, you can move off when you like. I'm leaving a clock here on top of this crate. It's twenty-five minutes past eight now. You should have enough air down here to keep you alive for two hours, and you won't need that much, will you? We wouldn't want you to suffo-cate. That's an ugly way to go. So there's just a hundred minutes to wait for a moment of history, gentlemen. God save Ireland!'

After those heroic sentiments, Cribb's final sight of Devlin before the hatch was sealed was the seat of his trousers moving upwards to freedom. The sound of the lid closing reverberated through the submarine boat.

Painfully, Cribb lifted his head to see whether McGee was equal to the task of moving the boat into position. He had appeared to understand Devlin's instructions, but could he function independently?

The answer was not long in coming. McGee leaned forward and pulled a lever. The boat began to move through the water. Cribb heard water churning into the ballast chambers beneath him. The submarine boat dipped below the surface. In a few seconds they surfaced, presumably to get a sighting of the pier through the scuttles, and then they submerged again in the approved 'porpoising' mode of navigation. The effort of concentration going on in the few functioning parts of that shattered brain must have been prodigious.

The vessel surfaced twice more, taking the long, low dive that meant McGee was moving it towards its final berth below the pier. It powered steadily ahead for seven seconds before he shut off the engine. The vibration wracking Cribb's body stopped. They glided silently forward for an interval too charged with tension to estimate accurately. Then there was a muffled bump. Another, stronger in impact, caused the boat to lurch towards starboard, before righting itself. A case of dynamite slid across the space behind McGee and stopped on the opposite side of the deck. The submarine boat was stationary. They were resting on the bottom of the Thames. Somewhere above them was Gravesend pier, decorated with the flags of the Empire and His Royal Highness's personal standard.

Cribb peered at Thackeray to see whether the jolting of the boat had made any difference. It had not.

The situation, then, was clear. A cynic might have described it as desperately clear. They were sealed from outside help by three fathoms of water. There was no chance at all of Cribb releasing himself from his bonds: he might as well have been wearing a strait-jacket. He would get no help from McGee. Thackeray was insensible, and tied hand and foot like himself.

Not quite like himself. They had not bothered with the additional constraint of the two straps about the arms, perhaps because they recognized that the chloral was more than enough to incapacitate him. He was bound around the ankles and wrists.

By turning on his side and leaning forward, Cribb could see the face of the clock Devlin had left behind. Five past nine. If his only hope of release was Thackeray's emergence from oblivion, then he *had* to assume that the constable would show signs of life at some stage. In the mean time it was sensible to employ himself trying to make some impression on the knots securing Thackeray's wrists. When his assistant *did* come round, every second, every loosened strand, would be vital.

How would he do it? With his teeth. Thank the Lord for a decent set of grinders!

First it was necessary to move Thackeray on to his side, no easy achievement with a sixteen stone man. It was no use nudging him fitfully with the knees. The job required leverage. He obtained it by planting his feet against the stanchion to which they were tied and wriggling into a position where his thighs were pressed against his chest and his left shoulder was wedged under Thackeray's right hip. By bracing his legs he succeeded in pressing the constable's substantial form so hard against the side of the boat that it was forced to turn. Once the right hip was pushed off the deck, it was like rolling a log. Thackeray's face turned to the wall and his bound hands appeared from under him.

They were tied with rope lashed two or three times round each wrist and then wound repeatedly round both, before being brought between the hands to cross the ligature so formed and bind it laterally. The two ends were secured by a formidable knot. The only encouraging thing about it was that it was in a position where Cribb could work at it with his teeth.

After twenty minutes, he had made no impression at all. It was Devlin's handiwork, he decided. A boatman's knowledge of working with rope, and a hammer-thrower's strength is a redoubtable combination. In the next ten minutes, however, he succeeded in loosening and separating the first join in the knot.

There was also a change in the rate of Thackeray's breathing, but whether it indicated returning consciousness or mild suffocation from lying face and beard downwards was difficult to estimate.

Twenty-five minutes to ten. Above them, the final arrangements for the Prince's reception would be under way. Roads adjacent to the river would be closed to traffic and the inspection party would be parading on the pier, with the Gravesend silver band tuning up in the background.

He applied his teeth to the next section of the knot and worried it like a terrier, his lips smarting from contact with the rope-fibres. It came away more readily. Encouraged, he jerked the ends clear and shifted the angle of his head to meet the new formation. It was slower to yield, but he worked it loose by sheer persistence.

Ten minutes to ten. The simple reef knot towards which he had been working was now revealed. He fastened his teeth on the part affording the best grip and doggedly disengaged it. He had mastered Devlin's knot!

As if in tribute, Thackeray emitted a long, low groan.

Five to ten.

'Thackeray! Can you hear me?'

No response.

There was still the binding round the wrists to loosen. Cribb switched his attention back to it, displacing it thong by thong to reveal the weals where the rope had bitten into Thackeray's wrists. When the last piece fell away and the hands separated, the constable groaned again.

Ten o'clock.

To quicken the process, Cribb leant forward and sharply nipped the tip of Thackeray's right forefinger with his teeth.

'Hey!' said Thackeray.

Cribb gripped the constable's sleeve in his teeth and rolled him on to his back. 'Wake up, man!'

Another groan.

Somewhere deep beneath them, an engine started to vibrate. McGee had switched on the pumps to eject water from the ballast chambers. The submarine boat was about to rise from the river-bed to nestle under the pier itself. By now the Royal carriage must have disgorged its Passenger.

He would be strolling over the gangway to meet the assembled dignitaries of Gravesend.

'Look sharp, blast you, you old perisher!' Cribb said.

'Whassat?' Thackeray's eyes opened – and closed again.

'You've got to untie me, man!'

'Untie me, man,' repeated Thackeray.

He looked at the clock.

It was five past ten.

The moment when, by all calculations, the course of history should have been altered. All calculations, that is to say, except Sergeant Cribb's.

It was five past ten and the detonation should have taken place, but Cribb had made quite sure that the Person Who Mattered was in no danger.

The urgency in what was happening under the pier had nothing to do with history. It was simply that Cribb did not intend to suffocate. If Thackeray could be persuaded into consciousness, he would certainly share the intention. Besides, it was unthinkable to be robbed of the pleasure of telling Inspector Jowett how a humble sergeant had foiled a Royal assassination.

On Devlin's reckoning, there was now enough air left to last them twenty minutes.

Cribb leaned over Thackeray. 'You're lying in a steel coffin fifteen feet under the Thames.'

'Eh!' Thackeray sat bolt upright.

'Release me, man, as quick as you can!' said Cribb.

It cannot be a pleasant experience to nod off after breakfast and wake up with your head pounding and your feet tied together, in an ill-ventilated submarine boat stacked with dynamite. It says much for Thackeray's quick response to the call of duty that he carried out the order without a word.

The straps proved harder to remove than the ropes, but a few choice exhortations to Thackeray assisted his efforts. Free at last, Cribb rubbed his wrists to restore the circulation. He looked at the clock.

Ten past ten.

It happened that in the moment he chose to look in that direction, he took in McGee in the same glance. The dynamiter, too, had taken note of the time and the apparent failure of Cribb's infernal machine. He had taken a box of matches from his pocket. He had struck one and was holding it over the nearest open crate of dynamite, waiting for the flame to catch enough of the match to ensure that it would not go out.

'Hand me a strap,' Cribb ordered.

Thackeray put one in his hand and he swung it high and with all the force at his command. It whipped down on McGee's forearm and encircled the wrist. Cribb tugged it back towards him at the same instant, jerking the arm away from the crate. The match fell on the deck and Cribb swept forward and stamped it out. He lifted McGee from the pilot's seat and laid him on the ground.

'Put the strap round his arms, Thackeray, and get the matches away from him,' he ordered. 'I'm going to try to take us to the surface.'

The difficulty in taking the controls was that he had heard the instructions without seeing which levers served the appropriate purposes. He looked through the glass to see how close they were to the pier. McGee had done his piloting well; the shadowy underside, fringed with weed, was directly overhead. He found the twin levers controlling the ballast chambers and admitted enough water to take them a fathom down. The lever in the centre, he judged, would start the propeller. It did. The submarine boat moved forward and clear of the pier. He switched on the pumps and they slowly ascended.

15

Thames water was still pouring off the susperstructure of the boat when Cribb thrust open the conning-tower lid and looked out. The early mist had given way to a clear, cloudless morning, the waves catching sunlight at a million shimmering points. Thirty yards to the left, the Imperial bunting fluttered bravely from a canvas awning specially erected on Gravesend pier. A trombone flashed as the band dispersed across the gangway. Red, white and blue streamers wreathed serpentine shapes in the current.

The thousand-yard width of Gravesend Reach was studded with river traffic, dominated in midstream by the gleaming lines of the *Hildegarde*. She was flying the Prince's standard. The launch which had conveyed him safely across the water was moored alongside. A flotilla of smaller craft cruised interestedly around her.

Somewhere on this stretch of river were the dynamiters, Cribb was confident. Carse would not forgo the pleasure of witnessing the climax of his plan. They would have been skirting the attendant fleet while the ceremonials took place on the pier, smug in their knowledge of what was under the water. And when their expectation was not realized at the proper time, they would have clenched their teeth and cursed clocks that could not be relied upon. If the machine that had blown up the gazebo had been marginally late in operating, perhaps this identical one was going to be the same. Even as the Royal feet had stepped over the gangway to the launch, the dynamiters must still have watched for what might appropriately be called the upshot of their plans. And if Cribb was any judge of human nature, they would be lingering on yet, looking for some indication of what had gone wrong.

Well, now they had got it. The emergence of the submarine boat told them for certain that the charge had failed to detonate. Not only that; they knew now that the law was bound to pursue them, for Cribb and Thackeray must have survived. Carse would swing the launch towards Northfleet and race upriver on the best head of steam he could raise. There was a good chance of reaching the house by the river and escaping in a carriage before Cribb could muster a posse to pursue them.

It was going to take time to go about it in the orthodox way, he was forced to admit. A request for reinforcements from Gravesend police station would want some explaining when it came from a man in a submarine boat with no identification whatsoever, claiming to be a police officer. An enlightened duty sergeant might be prepared to be convinced after, say, ten minutes of hard talking, but Cribb could not afford to give the dynamiters such a start.

No. He would finish this as he started it: in style.

There was one dependable way of collecting police reinforcements quickly and without argument. He put down the lid of the conning-tower and switched on the propellers, at the same time turning the wheel to set the submarine boat on a course directly in line with the *Hildegarde*. Devlin had been right: she was a capital craft, easy to handle and quick to accelerate. With the wheel held steady, he opened the ballast chambers and took on enough water to submerge the hull, leaving only the conning-tower visible above the waves.

A hundred yards from the yacht, he surfaced again, gliding audaciously through the inner circle of vessels in support. Through the glass scuttles he noticed a movement on the *Hildegarde*'s deck; two figures in blazers and white flannels had appeared there, and one was pointing in the direction of the submarine boat. His companion, broadly-built, with neatly-barbered beard, turned to say something to two young women who had appeared behind them with parasols. The prettier of the two stepped forward and linked her arm in his. Cribb swung the wheel to turn the boat in the direction of Northfleet, and discreetly submerged.

When he surfaced two minutes later, he was gratified to see that his strategem had worked; he now had an escort of three Thames police launches. He switched the engine to full power.

He sighted the dynamiters about 150 yards ahead, gaining what help they could from the tidal current. He would have spotted them earlier if his visibility had not been impaired by the thickness of the glass he had to peer through. He put up the lid of the conning-tower and stood on the pilot's seat for a better view. He could see Millar on deck, facing his direction, undoubtedly keeping the others informed of the progress of the pursuers.

Cribb was trying to recognize the others – and reflecting that Rossanna, at any rate, should be encouraged by the reappearance of the submarine boat – when, quite unexpectedly, a voice addressed him.

'Ahoy there! This is a river patrol of the Metropolitan

Police. You are showing no markings. Heave to, and identify yourself.'

The instruction had reached him through a megaphone, held by an officer of Thames Division, wearing the white boater trimmed with blue that was conceded as more appropriate to activities on the river than a regulation helmet.

'Declare your identity,' repeated the officer through the hailer.

Lord! This was the very thing he had sought to avoid. It was out of the question to stop, much as one regretted defying another member of the Force.

He waved back in as cordial a manner as he could, pointed meaningfully towards the dynamiters, and put down the hatch. Thames Division's launches were built for speed, but he doubted whether they could do anything to stop the submarine boat at its present rate of progress, with the Edison-Hopkinson motors running at some 750 revolutions a minute.

Besides, he was gradually reducing the stretch of water between the dynamiters and himself. It was difficult to understand why, because a smaller craft like theirs ought to have moved more quickly through the water. At this rate, he would be level with them before they entered Fiddler's Reach. Steadily he bore down, with the police launches still in escort and exasperatingly declining to chase the dynamiters.

A hundred yards soon became seventy, and seventy, fifty. Already he could see Carse at the wheel and Devlin beside him. Then the reason why the dynamiters had cut their speed was made clear. Millar, on deck, had levelled a gun at the submarine boat. They had deliberately allowed their pursuers to come within range.

A small puff of smoke was followed immediately by a sharp impact on the side of the conning-tower. It was aimed at the scuttles, and if Cribb took the boat any nearer, the next could not fail to find its mark. He swung the wheel to port and ducked his head low, as a second shot cracked against the plating on his right. Thank God for Siemens-Martin steel!

He heard two more shots discharged, and was comforted by the sound of one making contact harmlessly somewhere to stern, while the other seemed to have missed altogether. This encouraged him to raise his head and check his position in relation to the launch. The dynamiters were now slightly astern of him and fifty yards to starboard. Millar was still poised on deck, gun in hand, looking for a clear line of fire. The police, like Cribb, had swung defensively towards the Kent bank. There was no sign of the man with the megaphone.

What would Carse do now: move in to give Millar a better chance of a shot, or keep the same course, knowing his pursuers would have to stay out of range?

Cribb watched the bows of the launch, ready to react at once to any change of direction. And as he watched, there was an astonishing development.

Rossanna came running from the cabin and leapt into the river. With arms flailing, she struck out towards the submarine boat, her black cloak riding the water like a manta ray. Millar heard the splash, turned, took in what had happened and made rapidly to inform Carse, who shortly appeared on deck. Rossanna was already thirty yards astern, and he did not take long in deciding to abandon her. Cribb saw him shake his head curtly and return to the wheel.

Seconds later, the launch was ripped apart by a massive explosion. Cribb saw the flash and ducked instinctively. Fragments of wood and metal beat like hail on the hull of the submarine boat. Water cascaded across the scuttles, obscuring vision, and the whole vessel keeled dangerously to port, as the shock wave hit them.

The force of the explosion was indicated by the number of seconds the rain of debris lasted. Some of it must have blown two hundred feet in the air. Cribb turned off the engine and waited. When he raised the lid of the conning-tower, the water was black with Thames mud. Here and there, small splinters of white wood broke the still turbulent surface.

He looked for Rossanna and saw her cloak fanned out in the water not twenty yards from the boat. There was no sign of anyone else.

'Take charge, Thackeray!' he called down. He climbed up and dived from the conning-tower. He struck out with his powerful breast-stroke and soon had his hand on the cloak. Rossanna was underneath, on the point of sinking, too exhausted to continue the struggle. She had done amazingly well to stay afloat so long in her sodden clothes.

Holding her firmly around the diaphragm, he tugged the cloak free of her face and unfastened the bow at her neck. It had very likely saved her from being burnt and scarred in the deluge that followed the explosion. Strands of copper-coloured hair were adhering to her face, and he carefully lifted them clear and tilted her head to aid respiration. Then, moving his hands under her arms from the back, he placed them on her shoulders and drew her against his chest, in the life-saving position advocated by Lieutenant

Torkington in his *Swimming Drill*, and taught to such members of the Force as volunteered for aquatic training. He employed his legs to good effect, drawing the exhausted Rossanna easily through the water towards the submarine boat.

It was a shade disheartening to reach there and find that Thackeray had not had the foresight to put out the ladder from the conning-tower. He waited, treading water. After a quarter of a minute, he took a firm grip on Rossanna with his left hand, and thumped with his right on the metal hull.

There was no response from Thackeray. Blast it, the man must have fallen asleep again!

He changed his grip, and saw that Rossanna's eyes were open. 'Soon have you aboard, I hope,' he told her.

'The launch,' she said. 'Is it . . .?'

'Nothing left of it, Rossanna. What happened?'

'I saw them shooting at the submarine boat and I thought of all the dynamite in it, and my father helpless inside, and I couldn't bear it. I picked up a cake of dynamite from the case that was on the deck and dropped it in the bucket Patrick was using for the stoking. Then I jumped in the water.'

'You're lucky to be alive.'

'Is my father well?'

Cribb raised his eyebrows. 'But I gave you my word.'

'Of course.' Rossanna smiled.

'All right, mate, give us your hand, whoever you are,' called a sergeant of Thames Division, as their launch drew alongside. 'My mate says its Captain Webb, but I've got my money on Captain Nemo.'

Cribb helped Rossanna up, and then allowed himself to

be hauled from the water. He wiped the worst of the mud from his face and smoothed down his hair.

'As a matter of fact,' he said, 'I am Detective-Sergeant Cribb of Great Scotland Yard.'

'Well that bloody well beats everything!' said the sergeant.

Inspector Jowett refilled his pipe, stood up, walked thoughtfully to the window, was reminded that it was still boarded up from the Great Scotland Yard explosion, turned and resumed his seat. 'Truly an amazing story, Sergeant,' he said, lighting his pipe. 'I would have found it difficult to credit if I had not been down to Swanscombe Marshes myself to see where the submarine boat ran aground.'

'Ah, that was the result of a misunderstanding, sir,' said Cribb. 'Thames Division thought that Constable Thackeray was in control. He was asleep, sir. Effects of the chloral he was given. He can't be blamed.'

'My word, no!' said Jowett. 'I wouldn't dream of blaming Thackeray. First-rate man. I knew he was dependable from the start, of course. In my position, you have to know your own men, by Jove. Fundamental to the job.'

'So I believe, sir,' said Cribb.

'What you still haven't explained to me is how you did it,' Jowett continued.

'Did what, sir?'

Jowett put another match to his pipe. 'Well, you were given the job of constructing two identical infernal machines, one of which was to be used to demonstrate your skill as a dynamitard, while the other was afterwards put into the submarine boat. If I've understood your account of it correctly, you had no control over the selection of the bombs for these purposes, and the setting of the clocks was most stringently supervised.'

'Quite correct, sir.'

'So you couldn't have interfered with the machines after you had made them.'

'That's right, sir.'

'Yet the gazebo was blown to bits, while the bomb in the submarine boat failed to detonate. That's either extra-ordinary good luck or so ingenious that the explanation eludes me. I repeat, how did you do it?'

Cribb hesitated, tugging his side-whiskers, knowing, as conjurers do, that explanations add nothing to spectacular effects. He really could not refuse to answer Jowett's question, however. 'Well, sir. It was very simple. When I built the machines I made sure that *neither* of 'em would work. I carefully removed all the powder from the cartridges the pistols fired. So they couldn't go off, you see?'

'Frankly, I don't,' said Jowett. 'One of them destroyed the gazebo, so it must have gone off.'

'I'm afraid not, sir,' said Cribb apologetically. 'That box is probably still lying intact at the bottom of the lake. It was a straightforward charge of dynamite that blew up the gazebo. I removed a couple of bricks from the underside of one of the arches above the water and stuffed in several discs of Atlas Powder. Then I attached a piece of slow-match – that's a slow-burning fuse, sir – and gave it an hour. It was slightly late in working, but near enough to be convincing. That's a far more reliable way of blowing up a gazebo than using clocks and detonators nine feet under the water.'

'So that was it,' said Jowett, with disappointment in his voice. 'I thought it must be something cleverer than *that.*'

Cribb stoically accepted the rebuke. He watched Jowett make another attempt to light his pipe, before saying, 'I was rather wondering if you had any idea what would happen to Miss McGee and her father, sir.'

Jowett shook his head. 'Not much at all, Sergeant. From what you have told me, the major criminals perished in the explosion. Between you and me, there are reasons why it might be necessary to keep this case out of the courts altogether. The – er – party on the *Hildegarde* were blissfully unaware that the submarine boat was full of dynamite, and it is probably best all round if they remain unenlightened on that point. There is not much to be gained from bringing a helpless cripple like McGee before a judge, and his daughter seems to have played quite an insignificant part in the proceedings, from what you say. We'll keep an eye on her through the Special Branch, of course. Got to give those fellows something to occupy them, eh?'

'I suppose so, sir,' conceded Cribb, a little wistfully.

'I've got some capital news for you, though,' Jowett went on. 'Your work in this affair has not gone unrecognized, Cribb.'

'Really, sir?'

'Depend upon it, if a man in my charge does something as creditable as you have done, it gets reported to higher quarters.'

'Thank you, sir.'

'Yes, the Commissioner himself has heard about your exploits, and I believe he is more than a little impressed. He has gone so far as to make a personal recommendation, Cribb.'

Cribb came smartly to attention.

'He has recommended – and, of course, it has been

agreed by myself – that you be relieved from normal duties for the next three weeks to complete the explosives course at Woolwich Arsenal, which you had to leave prematurely. Congratulations! You will know more about explosives than anyone at Scotland Yard, Sergeant. You start tomorrow morning, at the point where you left off. Craters, I believe, and the effects of—'

'Blast,' said Cribb, with feeling.

HISTORICAL NOTE

With Sergeant Cribb's assignment completed, the reader might be interested to know some later developments in the actual events from which the story was projected.

The dynamite attacks on public buildings in London, which happened as described, continued into 1885. Three Clan-na-Gael agents were blown to pieces trying to destroy London Bridge from a boat; Gower Street Underground Station was attacked; and in three simultaneous explosions on January 24th, the White Tower of the Tower of London, Westminster Hall and the Chamber of the House of Commons were seriously damaged by dynamite. On April 23rd, a room in the Admiralty was bombed. The Special Branch made many arrests, and before the end of the year 25 dynamiters were imprisoned, 16 for life. By 1887, Scotland Yard had so far infiltrated the Clan, through such agents as Thomas Beach (alias Henri Le Caron) and 'Red' Jim McDermott, that a plot aimed to coincide with Queen Victoria's Jubilee was easily foiled, and the agents arrested.

John Holland's submarines, which began with sponsorship from the Skirmishing Fund, eventually became so respectable that the *Holland VIII* was recognized as the first reliable submarine in history and went into production for the US Navy in April 1900. Britain's first naval submarines, too, were Hollands, built by Vickers; and the German U-Boats, which brought Britain to the brink of defeat in the First World War, were built on the same principle.

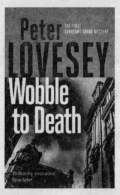

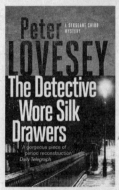

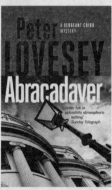

Discover Sergeant Cribb

'Lovesey has a special flair for re-creating Victorian England with to-the-manner-born wit'
Saturday Review

'Sinister fun in splendidly atmospheric setting'
Sunday Telegraph

'Delightful Victorian mysteries . . . [A] fine picture of vice, good mystery plotting, and fun'
San Francisco Chronicle